T0132176

Leash

Lea

JANE DELYNN

Semiotext(e)

Acknowledgements

SECTIONS OF THIS NOVEL WERE PRINTED IN <u>BAD SEX IS GOOD</u> (PAINTED LEAF PRESS, 1998), <u>BEST OF THE UNDERGROUND</u> (MASQUERADE, 1999), <u>BEST LESBIAN EROTICA 1998</u> (EDITED BY JENNIFER LEVIN & TRISTAN TAORMINO) AND <u>THE BEST OF BEST LESBIAN EROTICA</u> (CLEIS PRESS, 2000).

–

<u>LEASH</u>. COPYRIGHT ©2002 JANE DELYNN. EDITED BY CHRIS KRAUS. ALL RIGHTS RESERVED. PRINTED IN THE UNITED STATES OF AMERICA. NO PART OF THIS BOOK MAY BE USED OR REPRODUCED IN ANY MANNER WHATSOEVER WITHOUT WRITTEN PERMISSION EXCEPT IN THE CASE OF BRIEF QUOTATIONS EMBODIED IN CRITICAL ARTICLES AND REVIEWS.

–

FIRST <u>SEMIOTEXT(E)</u> EDITION PUBLISHED 2002

–

ISBN 978-1-58435-014-9

–

DESIGNED AT THE ROYAL ACADEMY OF NUTS + BOLTS, D.O.D. (WWW.THEROYALACADEMY.ORG). COVER ILLUSTRATION BY KATHARINE KUHARIC, COURTESY OF THE ARTIST AND P·P·O·W. GALLERY. BACK COVER PORTRAIT BY ROBERT GIARD.

–

<u>SEMIOTEXT(E)</u> PO BOX 629, SOUTH PASADENA, CALIFORNIA 91031

THANKS TO SEAN DEYOE FOR HIS CAREFUL AND CARING WORK ON THIS BOOK, ALSO TO SHANNON DURBIN, & ESPECIALLY TO CHRIS KRAUS, EDITOR EXTRAORDINAIRE – JD

For my dear friend Tsipi –
& (of course) Kate

Desire can never be satisfied,
because it is a desire to desire.
—Jacques Lacan

Leash

1.
What I Own

1

My Current having gone to Stockholm to research public housing over the summer recess, old longings began to stir. I had chosen, somewhat perversely, to remain in the city for the summer, for the sake, I now realized, of these strange longings. Our loft overlooked the Hudson River, and I remembered nights when we had first moved in, how I had gazed in envy at the men outside, walking, unspeaking, to their anonymous, compulsive rituals. The pier into which they vanished was long gone, and for a while, too, so were the men. But lately, in defiance of things rational, in grand indifference to what the rest of us pretend to hold so dear, in this the second decade of the Plague, men were again parading.

The old envy overcame me. I wanted to be out there, in a tee-shirt and torn jeans, 22.

If I could be a man for a night, or 22, which would I choose?

These were old thoughts, they belonged to another time, I had not expected them to flit through my brain again.

I turned the air-conditioner off and sat by the open window in the dark, my butt propped in a chair, feet on the windowsill, the moist air brushing my face. I could see the World Trade Center, I could see ochre and red lights appearing and disappearing in New Jersey (cars coming out of or going behind trees, etc.), I could see stars.

Divine, of course, but not what I wanted. I stuffed keys, cash, and my health insurance card into my shorts pocket and headed out.

2

The night was warm, moist, like the skin of an aroused woman, with a hint of fetid honeysuckle from the nearby pocket park. By the time I got to the bar the hairs nearest my scalp were wet. I did not mind. I like sweat, not so much on other people, but on me.

My love for bars is metaphysical and non-contingent. That is to say, it is in no way dependent on the kinds of experiences I have in them.

Outside, leaning against cars, groups of women smoked, chatted, flirted, though not with me. I pushed my way through them, unnoticed, to the entrance.

The room was small and narrow, painted in a kind of 1930s dark green, with a string of tiny white Xmas lights strung on the mirror behind the bar. These stayed up year-round, sometimes even with the fake frost still sprayed on the mirror, as if life were a perpetual holiday.

I walked to the rear, to the left of the piano. There was a table in a little niche in the corner. Two women sat next to each other, their heads at slight angles, mouths pressed to each other like the fish in the aquarium on the bar. I walked toward the empty chair at their table, but when I got there I did not sit down, but instead leaned against the wall.

A woman sat at the piano. In the mirror behind her you could see the strands of wet hair clinging to her neck. Her hands were moving and, like the fish and women kissing, her mouth was open. Out of it, in a somewhat hoarse and quavery voice which lent a spurious air of emotional resonance, came *I Fall to Pieces*. How to excuse myself? This particular song can bring tears to my eyes.

In recent years I have tried to switch from the concealment to the celebration of my jerkiness. I pushed my hands somewhat theatrically through my hair. When I let go, it immediately drooped back down over my eyes. For no reason I know of my hand grabbed my hair at the back of my head. Not knowing what to do with it, I brought my hand down to my side. As soon as I stopped thinking, I realized my hand was again running through my hair. Out of reflex (I'm sure) I started to grab the hair on the back of my head again.

Cool it. I told myself. *Jerk*.

I stared at the aquarium, pretending to watch the fish. They swam in and out of a little castle, amid a plastic fern and a stainless steel fork and spoon half-buried in the sand. A strand of pearls lay on the bottom too, reflecting the flashing Christmas lights. Of course, I *was* really watching the fish. But although they interested me, I felt it was under the pretense of a different sort of interest than the one I actually felt.

On the top of the piano was a big round globe with an opening at the top into which money could be dropped. In an equivalent male bar this would have been stuffed full of dollar bills, but because we were lesbians, financially-challenged and cheap, there were only a few quarters. I wanted to give the singer money, but didn't since everyone else was ignoring her.

I felt guilty about this, and obscurely embarrassed, both for her and myself.

I ordered a Heineken. My back against the wall, I drank it out of the bottle, tilting my head up as I swallowed it like a movie cowboy.

I stared at the women who had been kissing. Their mouths were no longer at cross angles. One was picking some skin from her cuticle. Tears were streaming down the face of the other. The lights of the bar were reflected in them, like the pearls in the aquarium. I was staring at these, rather than her, but when she noticed me watching she looked at me with hatred.

I understood, I sympathized, but still I watched. She got up and went to the bathroom.

Although the singer was in the midst of a Patsy Cline medley, I walked to the front of the bar, away from the piano. I stood by the door for a while. Nobody seemed to acknowledge I was famous or beautiful.

3

Coughing ostentatiously at the smoke, I stood outside to lean against a car. Several times I glanced at my watch with a look of distress, as if my date were late.

An attractive woman with streaked blonde hair wearing a skirt was tying the leash of her dog around a parking meter. It was a small terrier-like mongrel, somewhat too cute for my taste. "Hi doggie," I said, going over to pet it. The dog barked shrilly, then licked my hand. "What a cute dog," I lied.

"He's a good doggie too," she said, in that idiotic voice people talk about their pets. I knelt down to play with him/her. She went into the bar. After petting him/her for awhile, I stood up, stretched, and walked over to the window. The woman's back was toward me; she seemed engrossed in conversation with a black woman in an orange shirt.

I returned to the dog, to prove that was the real reason I had gone over to talk to the woman. I squatted on the pavement and scratched behind his/her ears. He/she jumped up, trying to lick my face. I kept him/her away with my arm, but could not prevent him/her from putting my hand in his/her mouth. Although I did not really like him/her, I let him/her do this, partly to maintain my charade of canine interest, and partly because (despite myself) I was flattered at his/her response.

After time enough to prove my canine interest had been genuine, I stood up and stretched. I looked at my watch and, loudly sighing for the sake of a group of women who were standing by the door, twisted my mouth into an irritated expression and (again) leaned against the car.

Three women crossed the street, laughing and falling against each other. One seemed to be looking at me. I gazed back at her with my most intense, eyes-narrowed look, willing her to leave her friends and walk over to me. She did not, and her eyes dropped mine at the time when she would have had to turn her head to continue looking. I walked to the corner, and watched them until they turned down the corner at Jane Street. Now their arms were around each other, and they began to sing. They had drunk too many beers, but they were happy. If I had drunk that many I would have been sad. Why was that?

With a final glance at my watch, I pushed myself off the car and walked back into the bar. The streaked-blond woman who owned the dog seemed to be staring in my direction, but to show her I hadn't played with her dog as a way to get to her I walked past her to the back of the bar, as if still looking for my phantom date. The two women who had been kissing, then crying and picking their nails, were now engrossed in conversation. The piano player was standing alone at the bar, drinking club soda. I felt sorry for her, so I told her I loved Patsy Cline.

"Dykes always do," she said. I was glad I had not left her any money.

I went over and stared at the fish, trying to think what to say to the blond woman. With a smile on my face I walked toward her. This time she was watching me, and smiled as I approached.

"*Honey*," she said, with an intonation similar to that of an old girlfriend.

"Uh...." I started to reach out to touch her arm, when the black woman moved past me with a pinkish drink and handed it to her.

I consoled myself by telling myself she wasn't really my type. Then I realized, she really *wasn't* my type. Not any more.

4

I walked down 12th to Hudson, then turned left. Do you want to know what I was thinking? I was wondering whether to go straight home or stop at the Korean deli to pick up some stuff I had meant to get this afternoon on the way home from the health club. Garbage bags, lemons, seltzer, fruit, salad stuff. Toilet paper and soap. Something else was there too, in the upper right-hand quadrant of my mind, a fuzzy space where a thought should be. I had had the thought this afternoon, standing at the sink, a brown paper bag in my hand, cleaning out the dish drain, plus the additional thought "remember it later."

It had been sunny when I had had my thought. The radio was on, a country song, I was feeling happy. The thought had pushed the happiness away – rather, put a slight cloud over it.

But maybe the cloud had been real, in the sky?

Oh yes, the carrot peeler. I had been wanting a new one for... years. Mine was spotted, aluminum, black. When I had had the thought this afternoon, I remembered previous times having had the thought, both at the sink and other places. That was the cloud.

In my mind was an 'ideal' carrot peeler, which the super-market never had, at least when I was there. I decided I would get one now, no matter what. I could always buy another one when I found myself at the 'ideal' household store. Was not perfectionism procrastination? By this act, I would, in the Kantian (categorical imperative) sense, reverse the sloth of a lifetime, as well as get rid of the space in my mind reserved for that thought, which in a sense was *always* there – not in the forefront, but like a pull-down menu on a mouse-driven program. On the other hand, with groceries I could not go to the other bar, which I suddenly realized had also been on my pull-down menu since even before I had left the apartment.

But maybe it was cute to go to the bar with groceries? Spontaneous. Would I not like someone like that?

Yes! I headed back to the store.

Again I stopped. Surely, after the bright lights of the market, the surfeit of stimuli of colored packages, I would lose the courage of my convictions. If I had left my apartment for pleas-ure, would it not show failure of nerve and will power to abandon that purpose now? Don't let the pleasure of duty interfere with the duty of pleasure.

I headed for the bar.

But I saw myself at the sink the next day thinking about the carrot peeler I had not bought. I saw the fatigue of 'carrot peeler' thoughts coming over me, the depression as I realized how I cluttered my mind. It was as real as the street I was walking on, more so maybe, for I could shut my eyes to an old man scavenging in a trash bin, but the carrot peeler was still in my mind.

Which would more likely conduce to the sum of human happiness – going to the bar or buying the carrot peeler? I no longer even considered the possibility of adding to human happiness by contributing to the scavenger (though sometimes, for no reason at all, I did).

Okay, I thought, I'll get the carrot peeler, and maybe a peach and plum or something for the morning.

I'll do both.

5

Tired and depressed from these thoughts (what we call thoughts – sentences and pictures), I was not really in a sexual mood. But I held a Beck's in my hand as I looked around the room.

The carrot peeler was in a little brown bag with several peaches and a plum on a shelf under a mirror opposite the bar. It was the same carrot peeler I had decided not to buy a few months ago. It was depressing to think I had had all these carrot peeler thoughts in the intervening months, only to end up with one I had recently rejected.

I decided that, having held out all this time, I should have continued to hold out until I got what I wanted. No doubt this was a moral useful in the bar as well.

Is it surprising no one came over to talk to me? Who wants to talk to someone who stands in a bar thinking about carrot peelers? I wouldn't have wanted to talk to me either.

This bar was noisier than the other one, the crowd younger and more interestingly dressed. Too interestingly dressed, in fact, for I was not sure I really wanted to lick an eyebrow that had an earring in it, let alone a similarly accoutred tongue or lip. Those who were not dressed as much as possible like teenage boys (tee-shirts, jeans, boots) were dressed as much as possible like teen-age girls (short skirts, heels, too much makeup). Because I no longer knew who I was, I did not know which of these types I was attracted to.

Or rather, because the point was not sexiness but the *iconography* of sexiness, I found myself attracted less to how someone looked than what their looks conveyed about they wanted me – their audience – to see them.

The room had a small but fairly crowded dance floor. The music alternated house and hip-hop to accommodate the divergent identities of the women therein: a politically pleasing conjunction of the affirmatively action challenged (white, Jewish) and *not* (black, Hispanic, Italian, Amer-Indian, Asian, or Cape Verdean – I am thinking of just *some* of the favored racial categories the Current had confronted during her job searches).

A woman with longish black hair came out of the bathroom. She leaned against the wall. Looking in the mirror, I could see she was looking at me.

Casually I turned from where I stood and stared at her. Then I turned back, and watched her make her way toward me in the mirror. I did not especially like the way she looked, but perhaps if I got drunk....

"You're a friend of Camille's, aren't you?" she said. "I think I saw you at her performance last week."

"No," I said. "I don't go to performances any more."

"I'm sure I saw you," she said.

"I don't think so."

We began to talk about art. She did some political-type installations dealing with racism, plus she was in an all-women's band. It was a downtown life, shared by probably half the people in the room. "I'm sick of the art scene," I said. "It's all bullshit. The only shows I go to are of really good friends."

She shrugged. The line wasn't very impressive, everybody had lots of artist friends. "What's your work like?" I finally asked, though I had vowed I would not ask such a question of anybody who did not ask it of me first.

She went into a song-and-dance about mixed media, photography, deconstructionism, etc. I'm sure you've heard it before. Nothing in the whole conversation, in fact, could possibly have been of any interest to anybody.

"What about you?" she asked.

"I'm a writer," I said, with my standard mixture of apparent modesty and concealed boastfulness.

She didn't ask me what I'd written. I decided I wouldn't volunteer. There's an age when you're flattered to have people go home with you because of who you are, and there's an age when you're more flattered if they go home with you because of how you look.

"Do you drink out of a bottle because you're butch?" she asked.

"Germs," I added, for I didn't want to make a stand one way or another on that issue. Her expression changed. "I don't mean AIDS," I explained. "But . . . anything." Men, after all, used this bar during the week.

The conversation faltered. Perhaps she was in ACT UP. "Are you very afraid of germs?" she asked.

"Yeah. In a way."

"So you practice safe sex?"

"Not really."

"Why not?"

"Well, for one thing I live with somebody," I said. "I mean, I was. I mean, she's away for the summer."

"You have an open relationship?"

"Sort of," I lied.

"And you don't think you owe it to her to practice safe sex?"

"I haven't really thought about it." We fell silent. Perhaps I was only reading disapproval into her expression. Although I knew lesbians who advocated practicing safe sex, I had never met one who actually felt it was necessary in her particular circumstances. "Why? Do you?"

"If I sleep with someone new. For instance, suppose we go home together. You could shoot drugs for all I know."

I held out my arms – a bit freckled from sun and age, but no tracks. "Not that I'm going home with you," I added. Until I heard myself, I had been thinking I would, but this remark put a pall over me.

"Why not? I like this song." She pulled me to her and started dancing. But my mind had wandered. I was thinking of an ex, I was even thinking of the Current.

I pushed myself away. "What's the matter with you?" she asked.

"I don't know."

Outside, I let my fingers dial (more by reflexive hand movements than memory) the number of the one before the Current.

"Carla?" I asked, when someone answered.

"Carla!" she called. "It's for you."

Fuck. I hung up.

On the way home I threw the carrot peeler in a garbage bin, though I kept the fruit for the morning.

6

I opened one of the two drawers under the platform bed. I fumbled behind the sheets to the place where I kept the toys and books.

I plugged in the vibrator. I turned on the tv. I turned off the lights.

7

The next morning, as I was downloading some e-mail, I idly flipped through *The Village Voice* Personals. You hear of people who have great success with ads, though you never actually meet these people yourself. I circled several of the more interesting ones.

On the way back from the health club I stopped at a place on Hudson Street where one can rent metal receptacles for the mail one chooses not to have delivered at home, either because of the person one lives with or because one does not desire to have one's address or telephone number known by one's correspondent.

At home I practiced until my voice sounded as casually

seductive as if I had not rehearsed at all, then I left the following messages:

Bored with ordinary things. Willing to experiment.

Jaded creative type in search of summer romance. If your photo pleases me, see how anxious I am to please you.

Looking for something. You tell me what.

Along with my postal box number and address, I included a request for a recent color photo.

I checked my mail drop every day. On the third I received a reply.

8

Dear Postal Box 504. If you are really anxious to please, my appearance should be irrelevant to you. The note was printed on a laser printer, and signed "Box 392."

At the pool in the health club, I invented responses. The task was so absorbing I lost track of the number of laps.

It should be, but it isn't. Send photo!

Are you famous (also), or just very ugly?

Sorry, kiddo, but I'm superficial as they come…come… come….

I walked home in a high in which the acrid swell of sweat mingled with the chlorine in a smell I would recognize anywhere. The sun on my eyelids burned orange even with my eyes shut, the air shimmered in the heat and light. I finally decided on the following:

Dear Box 392. Logic impeccable. Looking forward to further instructions. Anxious to please. Behind my apparent acceptance of her conditions was a secret hope that, being even wittier than I had at first assumed, she was in fact fabulous to behold.

9

Dear Postal Box 504, I read a few days later. *July ___ at 9 o'clock* (she gave an address in the East Village). *Ring the second bell from the top and go to the top. Not just the top floor, but right under the roof, and wait there for me.*

This was an amazing coincidence.

I voice-mailed back. *July ___ impossible. It's my birthday. Any other time. Your willing apprentice.*

Of course I wondered if she knew who I was, and had somehow picked this date on purpose. But how could she? Therefore, it was a sign.

I went downstairs and across the street to the pathway by the river. Women like me were walking their dogs. Some of them looked normal, some looked like women in the bar, and some looked extremely thin in their white tee-shirts, as if, like men, they too shot drugs, got hepatitis and AIDS. I felt torn between disgust and envy.

10

Saturday night I went to (yet) another bar, one on the bad (i.e. even worse) side of town. I scanned the faces wondering if one was hers. I formed an image of what she would look like: tall, thin, crewcut hair but with some odd thatch hanging down, perhaps dyed platinum, perhaps (but I hoped not) a pierced nipple or (even worse) nostril, with hairy, unshaven legs, wearing black leather shorts and black clunky boots with thick white socks. This is not an imaginative rendering, but an actual description of what a certain segment of the bar population looked like that particular night.

None of the women who looked like this seemed the slightest interested in me.

What if she doesn't like *me*? I thought. This possibility had not occurred to me before.

But how could someone *not* like me, who is (in some profound and subtle way I never stopped being astonished that people didn't notice) beautiful?

I did not normally sleep with people who looked like the women in this bar.

But what is 'normal'?

There was one person I found attractive. Her profile was just like a man's. Her hair was early Elvis. Her skin was white and unmarked.

A very handsome boy.

11

I plugged in the vibrator. I turned on the tv. I turned off the lights.

The image of young Elvis came to me. I turned off the tv. Lying on my back, I pictured myself lying on my stomach, Elvis on top of me, spreading my legs to do something unspeakable.

I am not interested in men, but sometimes I choose to sleep with women who look like men. (God knows you have told us often enough we are perverse, so you should not be surprised if we do perverse things.

Once you expect us to do them, alas, half the fun goes out of them.)

As Elvis entered, the memory of certain things I had done, a long time ago, returned to me.

12

I picked up the note the day before my birthday. *Dear Willing Apprentice. Change of plans impossible. Perhaps, after all, you are not so "anxious to please." Expecting you as planned.*

She was becoming more difficult. I decided I liked that; it was interesting and unexpected. Even if she *was* ugly, what would it matter for one night? I didn't have to see her again. I left a message on Leslie's machine canceling plans I had made for dinner the next night with her and some friends.

13

Although I had forsworn my late-afternoon espresso pick-me-up, I had trouble falling asleep. Somehow I had convinced myself she really *was* young Elvis, and though this was crazy, the possibility was sufficient to keep me awake, especially on a night when the light from the moon bounced directly in my eyes. Even with my eyes shut, I could feel it on my lids. I had an amazingly strong desire to shove my hand into my body, though "sex" seemed to have less to do with it than "anxiety" – as if only a fist could pummel my nerves into submission. But no fist was available, or rather – because I preferred to exercise my desire on a fist that was not my own and such a fist was not available – I decided to sacrifice an Ambien instead, one of my very few remaining.

The sacrifice bothered me, as did the "waste" of my sexual desire, which for me is not a renewable resource, like water, but more like oil: once used slow to replenish, worthy of depletion allowance (the pressure, once abated, needs time to build up again), etc. Thus my body (which craved immediate gratification) fought my brain (operating on the conservation of energy principle), and even with the pill, it took hours of position shifting and discarding and retrieving of sheet and comforter before I managed to slip into an intermittent and unsatisfying sleep – just the kind of night I did not want to have before the grand encounter.

But so often one gets what one consciously does not want, and does not get what one consciously wants, that one begins to wonder if there's a pattern to this, and what secret pleasure is to be found therein.

14

In the morning the sky was distant, the sun cold. I was cold too, though it could have been the Ambien, making me foggy and slow. My throat was dry, as if I had drunk too much, and my muscles were stiff, perhaps from the cold. Worst was a peculiar smell on me, almost of urine, which I was suddenly afraid would not wash off. I had been near people who had such odors, which seemed strangely resistant to water and soap. What if I were to be marked hereafter by some such smell, as old people and mothers are?

I was getting out of the shower when the Current (the one with whom I exchanged rings, the one whom, to be honest, I cannot swear I like) called, as she had warned me she would. It was, after all, my birthday.

As she chattered I stared at my drawings and paintings, most of which she co-owned, along with the 2300 square foot loft with the 11 foot high ceilings and eight 4' x 7' windows, the red leather chair with its matching leather couch, the Thonet chairs and Philippe Starck cabinet, the bed and night tables by Dakota Jackson, the Sub-Zero fridge and the Viking cooking range and the bathroom Jacuzzi, the paintings and drawings by Katharine Kuharic, Perry Bard, Martha Diamond, Bill Sullivan, Julia Kunin, Christo, Helene Aylon, Zoe Leonard, Sheree Levin, Donna Dennis, Judy Somerville, and Richard Dupont, the 54" Mitsubishi projection tv with digital picture-in-a-picture, the 36" Sony VEGA tv with digital PIP, two VCRs, 5 DVDs (3 of which are on computers and which have never been used), a Bang & Olafsen built-in stereo system, 5 CD changers (including ones on computers, portable radios and boomboxes), one mini-DV digital camcorder and one (old) analogue 8mm camcorder, 2 sets of cordless earphones and 2 universal remote controls, 4 computers (including a regular notebook and an ultra-lite), one black-and-white and one color laser printer, a flatbed scanner and a Visioneer Paperport scanner, 4 phone lines (two mobile and two regular), 1 plain paper fax, a dual-line T.A.D. and 2 two-line cordless phones, 7 phones (including the mobiles and ones on the plain paper fax), a cable modem, 200+ CDs, 300+ old record albums we couldn't bring ourselves to throw out (now hidden in a closet), uncountable numbers of tapes (both home-made and otherwise) – not to mention piles of cameras, portable radios, Walkpeople, binoculars, etc. too numerous to count.

Did these bring me happiness? Not at all. Yet I was sure I could not survive without them.

After the obligatory congratulations and an apology for not getting my present to me in time, the Current launched into a critique of my half of our e-mail correspondence, which she considered deficient in terms of frequency, duration, and the platitudes of affection.

Lying on my back on the bed, I dangled the phone a little above me in the air, so I would have to strain to hear the words. It was more interesting that way.

"Do you miss me?" she asked. The voice was far away. I brought it to my ear. "I asked if you missed me," she repeated.

"Of course," I sighed.

"Are you getting your work done?"

Another, even longer sigh. "No."

"So come join me."

"I'm not in the mood."

"You used to love to travel," she said plaintively.

"Not to Sweden."

"I thought you thought it was the greatest country in the world."

"Conceptually. To be honest, I'd probably rather live in South Africa."

A longer silence. "Are you ill?" she finally asked.

Although I'm sure she'd rather I be ill than prefer living in South Africa to Sweden, I said no.

After a long silence, she asked about Esmeralda. More than once we had reverted to "pet" discussion in preference to argument.

"She's fine." I got Esmeralda and held her ear up to the phone. "Say 'hi.'"

Esmeralda squirmed and I put her down. I listened for awhile as the Current mouthed inanities about "being a good girl . . . not knocking over the water bowl . . . . not scratching the couch," etc.

"People sound so stupid when they talk to their pets," I said.

"Fuck you." She hung up.

This little show of independence made me like her better, though not enough to call her back. But I thought about it, with the same kind of enjoyment I got on hot summer evenings when I lay in bed thinking about whether it was worth it to get out of bed, stumble over to the air-conditioner, and fiddle with the controls.

I decided it was a bad idea, as it would only reinforce her hanging up on me when she was angry, an action which, although I rather admired at the moment, would over time become melodramatic and tedious.

I burrowed through drawers until I found an old baggie with bits of dried twigs and leaves in it. My tampons now came encased in plastic, I could not find my rolling papers, so I took a pencil and wrapped aluminum foil around it, leaving some extra at the end which I fastened into a little bowl. I stabbed the bowl several times with the point of a knife, then, having placed some twigs and leaves into the concavity, and discarding the pencil, I held the hollow tube to my mouth and lit a match. After which I inhaled the only illegal substance the government had ever managed to get even somewhat under its control – as demonstrated by the extraordinary sum I was forced to pay for my quarter ounce.

It felt pleasant, as if I were a criminal – especially because I was not in some East Village dump, but in a loft most people I knew would kill to be in.

But although they would kill to be in it, if they were here they wouldn't have smoked dope with me, as most of them were in programs to help keep themselves free from various addictions (but not from the addiction of the programs themselves.)

Nonetheless, because they still lived in the East Village, because in years or decades past they had staggered down the street, because they had awoken covered in vomit in the apartments of strangers whose names they did not know, they still thought of themselves as criminals and me as bourgeois, though probably the only criminal thing they had done in years was underpay their income taxes.

But what poor person can underpay their income taxes as much as I can?

I realized I was humming "Mr. Soul" under my breath. I searched for it among the records we kept hidden in the closet for just such moments. I had not played it (or perhaps any record) in years. It was scratchy and full of hisses. I reminded myself there had been a time, not so long ago, that I could listen to entire stacks of records filled with scratches, through a 25-watt amplifier hooked up to speakers that cost perhaps a tenth of what mine (ours) did, and enjoy it utterly.

Such philosophizing helped me to enjoy it (if not *utterly*), but I made a mental note to buy the CD the next time I went to Tower Records.

Thus it is that Capitalism encases us in its chains. Does not every phone call the T.A.D. records, every program one buys for one's computer, every hunk of frozen meat one feeds to one's microwave, serve to enslave us further?

But if I were not enslaved, could I want anything?

I realized I was hungry, and made some tuna fish.

15

Before leaving the apartment, I put the various notes I had received, along with *The Village Voice* ad and receipt for the P.O. box and the East Village address to which I was going, in a 10" x 13" manila envelope I sealed and left by the door. On the front I wrote in a thick black permanent marker "In case something happens to me." I wore khaki twill shorts, a new short-sleeved off-white shirt of an astonishing weave and price, and expensive sandals with molded rubber soles. With great trepidation (lest I have a heart attack, be hit by a car, be chopped in pieces, etc.) I left my health insurance card at home, though I carried (both for a good luck token and to help in case of amnesia) a matchbook of a restaurant one block west of where I lived.

Having debated (and rejected) bringing flowers, out of fear it would signal *bourgeois*-ness or sentimentality, rather than irony, I bought a six-pack of Rolling Rock – a deliberately anonymous beer, for I wanted to confine whatever quirkiness I possessed to a single sphere. But near her building I abandoned it, partly because it might give a faulty impression of nervousness and/or alcoholism, and partly because she might be in AA, like everybody else in the East Village.

Two Spanish men eyed my abandonment of the six-pack with suspicion. Halfway down the block I turned; they still had not retrieved it. Though they were looking at me looking at them, I walked back and got it.

16

Not just the outer but the inner door was unlocked, as they often are in crummy tenements.

I walked up the stairs, indented in the middle from decades of footsteps, walls bumpy from ancient attempts to make the "texture" interesting – paint chipped, graffitied, peeling, names of old lovers (*Mike & Cathy forever*, *Julio loves Sandy*) etched by key or knife into its surface. Garlic, marijuana, fried chicken, rotting food – Spanish music and kids screaming and tv in various languages mingling in a way that was pleasantly familiar. In the past I had known buildings like this so well, with their geographically-labeled (NE, SE, NW, SW) apartments, the chains through which old ladies peeked before opening the door, the tied-up bags of garbage (brown bags inside of plastic) waiting outside doors to be carried downstairs – all the joys of downward mobility, whether involuntary or chosen.

I went up the stairs as far as I could until I faced a metal door to the roof. I assumed this was where I was supposed to wait, and I put the six-pack down. On the floor was a little brown paper bag, on top of which was a printed note that read: *Put this on.*

Inside the bag was a kind of large blindfold, almost a partial hood, of black leather, with an arched area to go over one's nose and what felt like real fur behind the eyepatches. The back was a thick band of elastic, but there were also velcro straps to make it even tighter.

Feeling stupid, but also intrigued, I placed the blindfold over my face. In my life, of course, I have had occasion to make use of blindfolds, but none this elaborate or so intelligently designed. Once on, there was no way to dislodge it to catch a glimpse of anything; in any case, the tickling of the fur on the eyeball made it impossible to open your eyes for more than a second.

As I waited, I leaned against the wall, stiffening and relaxing various muscles of my back so that the pressure of the wall worked against them almost like a massage. Then somehow, despite my curiosity and nervousness, I grew sleepy, as has happened more than once in a dentist's chair. Ignoring my concern re my twill shorts, I sat down on the floor.

"Is the blindfold on?" a voice startled me.

"Yes," I said truthfully, though my heart pounded as if I had been caught lying.

"How much can you see?"

"Nothing."

"Good. Stand up, but keep your back toward me." A bit awkwardly, for I was still startled by the intrusion of her voice inside my unconscious, I pushed myself to my feet. "Now reach out with your left hand, until you feel the banister."

I fumbled around, my palm against the wall, until, reaching backward, I felt the metal railing, cool and knobby from decades of paint.

"Good. Now move over...more...more...a little backward...Stop. The stairs are right behind you." I shuffled my feet very slowly until I could feel my heel sliding off the edge of the step. "Good. Now lift your right foot and place it behind you.

Hold on tight so you don't fall, and walk slowly down the stairs."

"Backwards?"

"Yes."

Even though her voice came from below me, I was scared somehow she'd push me. "What if I break my neck and become paralyzed?"

"You won't."

"But what if I do?"

"You won't."

"What about the beer?"

She laughed. "We won't need it."

'I don't need any of this,' I told myself, but nonetheless I let my left hand slide slightly down the banister, which was now becoming wet from my sweat and, gripping it hard as I could, reached behind me with my right leg until I found the lower step.

Carefully shifting my weight onto this leg, I fumbled in the air with my left leg. Thus, proceeding cautiously, but slightly faster, like a precocious child learning to walk, I made my way down the stairs.

"One more step," she said. I lowered my foot, then a jarring went through my body, as my foot landed unexpectedly on the floor.

She turned me around, so her voice was in front of me. "What do I look like?"

"I don't know."

She laughed, then placed one hand on my right shoulder, and one on my left arm, and pulling with one arm and pushing with the other, began to spin me around. Then she removed her hands and told me to do this myself until I got dizzy. When I stopped she took me by the hand and told me to follow her.

"Where are we going?" I resisted.

"You'll...*see*."

"Will I?"

"Don't you trust me?"

"I don't know."

I tried to figure out which way I was facing, but the spinning had confused me. I liked the feeling of my hand in hers, though, and the quality of her voice, which was musical but slightly husky, as if she were thirsty, or getting a cold, or had talked all day on the phone.

She stopped. I heard a slight creak (a door being pushed open), then, after warning me to lift my foot a little, my foot landed on a somewhat softer and more absorbent surface, which I realized was wood, and then I realized what I had been standing on before was tile.

I felt wind, I heard a kind of aching sigh, I heard the click as she turned the lock on the door.

17

"No!" She grabbed my arm, for I had unconsciously reached for the blindfold. "You're to leave this on, until I tell you you can take it off. Is that understood?"

"Yes."

"If you disobey me, you'll have to leave." Her hand was strong, and I felt like doing what she wanted.

She let go. I stood there, heart pounding, my breathing loud in my ears, like my grandmother's used to be when she slept in my room. At the time, it had made me want to kill her.

There was a long silence, during which I grew more and more nervous. Had she left the room? I crossed my left leg behind my right and began the process of lowering myself to the floor, much more difficult than you'd imagine without the visual clues.

"What are you doing?" Again the voice seemed to come from inside my head.

"I'm tired of standing."

"I didn't tell you you could sit down, did I?"

"No."

"So get back up."

I got up.

"You do only what I tell you to do, and don't do anything unless I tell you you can."

"Okay." I stood a while more. Sweat was emanating from me, not from any particular place but in a kind of suffused oozing. The floor creaked.

"What's your name?" she asked.

"Chris," I said after a pause.

"Chris *what*?"

"I don't want to say."

"Is 'Chris' your real name?"

"No," I admitted.

"What's your real name?" I was silent.

"Oh, you're one of *those*," she said. "You'll learn soon enough." A long pause. "Chris," she said, exaggerating the 'Chris,' "it's warm in here, don't you think?"

I shrugged. "It's okay."

"Well, *I'm* warm." Pause. "Would you like to take off your shirt?"

"Uh. Sure."

I began unbuttoning my shirt. Never having worn it before, I had trouble getting the buttons out of the buttonholes, which made me self-conscious (lest she think I was nervous), so I tried to move faster, which made me more clumsy. Finally, I got it off. Not wanting to discard it, I held it in my left hand. How much did it weigh? Six ounces?

I was very conscious of my erect nipples, with little bumps from cold, or arousal, on them.

"Drop it."

"It's ... clean." (I didn't want to admit it was new.)

Snicker. I let go. "No bra."

"No. I ... I used to have small breasts. Not that they're big now, exactly, but I keep forgetting."

"You forget?"

"In the store I mean. I haven't bought a bra in ... so long. Do you think I should wear one?"

"I've got nothing against tits. But it might look better with your new shirt."

"The shirt's not new," I protested. "I mean, it is, but I didn't buy it for you."

"I didn't think you did."

"Not that I wouldn't," I added.

"Do you buy a lot of clothes?"

"Yes. I mean no. Not really. It depends."

"I see...."

She continued questioning me in this calm and impersonal manner, as if at a doctor's office. The calmness was reassuring, though it gave me the feeling she was disappointed in my appearance. But perhaps she was merely nervous about how I'd feel about hers.

I could both hear and feel the floor move as she approached. I smelled her body, her breath, even a bit of her armpits.

I waited, but she did not touch me. If she had, perhaps I would not have begun to get wet.

"Can I take the blindfold off now?"

"No."

"When can I?"

She moved away, with her breath and warmth. "Please finish getting undressed."

'*Please*': what did that mean? I didn't know the rules. Would she say, in the same neutral voice, '*please* bend over so I can shove a dildo up your butt?'

I unbuckled my brown leather belt, unbuttoned the top of my shorts, unzipped the zipper. The shorts began to slip off, and I grabbed them.

"Let go," she said.

But I wouldn't, even though the keys fell onto the floor. I resisted an intense urge to bend down and feel for them.

"What's the problem?"

I did not want to put the idea of running off with my clothing into her head, if it was not there already. "I've never done any thing like this before," I finally said.

"You've never taken off your shorts in front of another woman?"

"You know what I mean."

"Do I?"

We were silent awhile. The ticking, was it my watch? "I...I'm scared," I said.

"Of course." Silence. "What are you frightened of?"

"I don't know."

"Come *on*."

"Being hurt, I guess," I finally said. But that wasn't it, exactly.

"Chris." She said it reproachfully, almost sadly. "You do know that some of the things we might do together might hurt you, don't you? That's partly why you're here, isn't it?"

"I suppose."

"Now let go of your shorts."

I did.

"Quite the little femme," she said, I suppose in honor of the lacy black underpants I had bought from Victoria Secret in honor of our 'date,' and which I now regretted.

"I'm not sure what I am," I replied.

"Perhaps we'll find out."

More time passed. I have never been able to stand being stared at. "I think we've admired your underpants enough," she said.

"Huh?"

"You can take them off."

"Oh. Yeah."

But this was hard to do, as the shorts around my ankles prevented me from raising my leg to pull them off, or even kick off a sandal. After several failed attempts, and almost falling over, I started to sit down.

Then I remembered her irritation when I had done this before. "Is it okay if I sit down?" I asked, almost hopping on one leg.

"You may." I sat down, pulled off my sandals, then my shorts, then raised myself up enough to slip off my underpants. She told me to get up again.

I was barefoot and naked. Although she had told me to keep my hands by my sides, they kept wandering to cover my breasts, as if I were Eve and had just eaten the apple.

"This is really embarrassing," I said.

"Turn around so I can see the rest of you. Slowly."

As I turned, I felt awkward and unattractive, the parody of a model. For all I knew, there were no blinds on the windows, and people in the apartments across the street could see me too. "Spread your legs." Her voice was very close to me now.

I could feel the gunk between my thighs stretch, then break.

"My my." I felt her fingers slightly touch the hair around my vagina, or rather, as hair has no feeling, I felt the pressure of the hair against the follicles. Each movement seemed huge, but slow, like under a magnifying glass, and so the mere proximity of her hand slightly above my skin warmed me and made me get wetter and wetter. Moving slightly, as if to shift weight, I moved my legs slightly further apart, willing her to put her fingers or even her hand inside.

Instead, she stroked my face with her fingers – her fingers that were wet from my gunk – and in the breeze from the window or fan the gunk dried into a mask.

She stuck her fingers in my mouth.

"Do you like to taste yourself?"

"Sokay."

If I was excited sucking her hand it was not so much because of what was happening as because it reminded me of something I had seen in a porno movie. The predictability of my response, to such a conventional action, annoyed me.

She removed her hand from my mouth and returned it to my pubic area.

"God," I said. "Oh God."

"Surely you're not going to come," she said.

"*Jesus*." I bit my lip. I was dripping. 'I haven't felt like this before,' went through my mind, though of course it wasn't true. I was moaning. I wanted to howl.

She withdrew her hand. "Don't stop," I begged.

"I don't want you to come."

"I can't help it. Oh god..." I grabbed her hand and tried to shove it in my vagina. "*Please*."

She grabbed my left arm and twisted it behind my back. "Who makes the rules around here?"

She turned me so my back was toward her. Her right hand moved around my body to grab my right nipple. She squeezed it between her thumb and finger. At first this pressure felt good, because the pain distracted me from my desire, then the pain itself became a problem. "Ow," I said. "Ow... ow." She put her left hand around my neck and yanked. My feet slipped and I was leaning against her. At first I resisted, but she was stronger than me; I relaxed and let myself sink into the pain. It was so deep it was no longer connected to the nipple, but spread in waves throughout my entire body. Somehow it didn't matter. Then she began twisting her hand, and the pain was again sharp and discrete, as if an ice pick were going through the center of my nipple. I became worried, not about the pain, but that she might do permanent damage to my nipple.

As I tried to pull away, she grabbed my left nipple with her left hand. This fresh pain distracted me from the old one. Then she let go of the left and squeezed with her right. Soon this alternation of pain itself became a rhythm, and I again relaxed.

She dropped my right nipple, grabbed my hair, pulled my head back, and sucked, really hard, on the side of my neck. It would be a gigantic hickey. Then it became a bite. I felt like she was eating me. Like she was an animal. "Ow. Oh. Ow." Her teeth dug into me. What if she drew blood? Wasn't she worried about AIDS?

She stopped for a minute. She pulled back my hair, so my throat was exposed to her.

I wanted her to bite it, suck my blood, make me part of that strange race.

She pulled my hair harder. "So Chris, does it matter what I look like?"

"No."

18

She placed straps around my wrists, also lined with what seemed like fur, then attached these to each other, so my hands were yoked together. She had me lie down on a surface that, from its scratchy feel and smell of dead skin and fecal matter of dust mites, had to be a couch, then attached the straps to something over my head, so my arms were stretched out above me.

She ran her hands up and down my body, not sexually so much as in examination. She commented on the hardness of my nipples, and the way the various parts of my body seemed to rise to meet her hands, even when (or especially when) she commanded me to lie still.

"Do you always get aroused so easily?" she asked, almost critically.

"Not *always*, no. But then, I'm not usually tied up naked with someone I've just met."

"Not 'usually,' but 'sometimes'?"

"No. Never."

"That's hard to believe. You seem to do this so ... *naturally*."

"My girlfriend's away. I'm ... bored."

"So you are a cheater. Maybe a hypocrite too?"

Her intonations were odd, like a foreigner translating. Then I realized she had an accent. Could she have had one before and I somehow not noticed? It is amazing what one misses sometimes. People with webbed hands, cauliflower ears, huge breasts....

I felt a shock to my face. It took me a second to realize what it was. "When I ask you something, answer it."

"You slapped me," I said, in a surprise that was not really a surprise.

It happened again. "Answer me."

The question was far-off, lost in an odd peacefulness of returning to ... something.

"I'm a hypocrite. A cheater," I remembered with effort.

She pinched my nipples. "They're erect."

"Yes."

"Is that a sign of arousal or of fear?"

"Arousal. Well, both," I admitted.

"And why is that?"

"You know."

"Do I?"

"Anything could happen, you know...."

Silence, then a thoughtful, "Yes. Yes, it could."

There was a longer silence. I was not bored by it – it seemed rich and full of meaning – but I wondered whether she was.

I felt something flick across my thigh, casually. It stung only a little. I sucked in my breath. She hit me again. I breathed even faster.

She touched a finger to the front of my vagina.

She laughed. "You're a regular gusher, aren't you?" she asked.

Again my mind wandered, and again she hit me. "Yes."

"Yes *what*?"

"Yes, I'm a gusher." Between the pain and the turn-on it was hard to talk.

"Quite the little slut, I get the feeling."

My ass twitched, at the word 'slut.' "A bit."

"You sound proud of that."

"No."

She hit me again.

"Maybe a little," I admitted.

"A little proud of being a slut? You don't sound like a very good girl, Chris."

"*Ow*. No."

"Does it hurt a lot?"

"No. Not really."

"Would you like it to hurt more?"

A thrill went through me. I couldn't say anything. She put the whip handle in my vagina. As she talked she moved it very casually in and out of me, like a dildo, but it was thinner and less satisfying. "Oh god, please." I was gyrating.

"I think you do want it to hurt more, don't you Chris?"

"No," I moaned.

My body kept trying to suck the whip handle inside. She played a game of just pulling it out of my body, then, when I had become resigned to this, pushing it back in.

Then she stopped. There was a thud. She walked away.

When she came back she ordered me to roll over on my stomach. In this position I became much more conscious of the nubby material and musty smell of the couch.

She sat down next to me, and told me to place myself across her lap.

I felt the roughness of her jeans and the pleasant coldness of the buckle of her belt against my skin.

"Do you know what I'm going to do?" she asked, gently stroking my ass.

"Spank me?"

"Perhaps. But only if you want me to. Do you want me to?" I was silent. "Come on, Chris."

"I don't know. It's up to you."

"Is it?"

I remained silent. She pulled apart my cheeks, as if inspecting me. She made little circles on my skin with her fingers. She smoothed my ass as if it were a wrinkled piece of paper. She rubbed the hairs on the back of my neck. Periodically she touched my vagina to check on its wetness. But she did not hit me.

"Well?" she said, after awhile.

"What?"

"You know."

"I don't."

"I think you do."

Finally I whispered: "spank me."

"I can't hear you."

"You can spank me," I said.

"Thank you, Chris, for your permission." She stopped touching me. The silence was very full. "*Please*," she said.

"*Please*," I repeated.

"Please *what*?" she asked.

"Please spank me."

"Why?"

"I don't know."

She waited awhile. I felt the smack, then heard it. The pain came a few seconds later.

"Ow," I said, more in surprise than anything else. "Ow." I realized I had been expecting her to use her hand, but it was something firmer, that hurt more.

After all this waiting, the strokes came fairly quickly and steadily. "Take it easy," I told her. "I won't be able to go to the health club."

"*That's* too bad."

Soon the pleasure of the novelty wore off, and the pain, which was both on the surface and somewhere deeper, took over, and I found myself moaning and begging her to stop.

After one particularly hard blow, I heard myself shouting "*Ow! Ow!*" not as before, but because I really meant it.

"If you make too much noise, Chris, I'll have to put a gag on you. You wouldn't like that, would you?"

"No."

"I wouldn't either. I wouldn't be able to hear these lovely cries."

She waited until I calmed down, then began to hit me again. I tried to curl myself around her legs, but she put one arm on my neck to hold me still.

"Oh God. Oh God." I bit my lip, then the couch, coating my lips with dust and the dried fecal matter of mites. "Stop! Please *stop*."

She did as I asked, and the room grew very quiet. "Do you really want me to stop, Chris, or is that part of the game?"

"I don't know."

She brushed my hair off my forehead, the way I like people to do. "Your safe word is 'red.' Say that and we immediately stop. 'Yellow' means what's going on is okay, but don't go any further. Okay?"

"Okay."

"Now Chris, that paddle is in my hand again. You know what to say if you don't want me to use it."

I didn't say anything. If this was going to be a contest of wills, I decided I'd win it. It really was not so difficult, if you went inside yourself. Then all of a sudden my stomach curled, as if I were going to vomit. "Yellow," I said. "Yellow." She hit me twice more, then stopped.

We sat there, unmoving. Then she placed her hand gently on my neck, my bottom, my back. My stomach calmed down. I slithered my head into her lap and began sobbing.

19

"On your knees," she ordered, when I was done.

"I can't." I was exhausted. I wanted to fall asleep, my head against her legs.

"You poor thing." She rubbed her hand through my hair, the way I train my lovers to do. "I need a smoke."

I lay there comfortably, half-drowsing, as she got up. A few minutes later I heard the match. I waited for the smell of burning paper and tobacco. The wax landed on my skin. It took a second before I recognized the sensation as pain. In surprise I giggled.

Wax on skin is one thing, but nipples another. As I was still screaming, she turned me over, pulled my legs up and apart so my ass was in the air, and pushed my head down onto my hands.

"Please," I whimpered.

"Your desires are irrelevant," she said, "and will be so long as I permit you to be with me. Do you understand?"

This was the same word she had used in her second letter ("if you are really anxious to please my appearance should be irrelevant to you") and the iteration of it evoked if not arousal then a memory of arousal, so that when she pressed the cool tip of the latex against my rectum, I was able to relax enough to allow the tip in.

She went slowly at first, and gently, spreading my cheeks apart with her hands, then without warning gave a huge push. Because I was insufficiently lubricated, my skin adhered to the latex; I worried my sphincter muscle would be ripped. Behind this sharp but circumscribed pain was a deeper and duller pain as my insides were filled, then behind this appeared a third even more diffuse pain that spread out over my entire consciousness so that soon it was no longer "pain" – just a background sensation against which the other smaller but sharper pains glowed like bright stars against the background of the Milky Way. The complexity of the sensations was so distracting that for a while I actually forgot that what I was thinking about was "pain."

She pushed my legs toward my head, so my ass was even higher in the air, and began a rhythmic pushing. "Uh uh uh uh," I repeated, like a mantra; the repetition of the words soothed me, almost as if it were someone else singing to me. She yanked my hair; again I kind of liked it, because the sharpness of the pain distracted me from the other, duller pain. The pulling got harder and my "ows" got louder, though I wasn't sure whether this was because it actually hurt more or because I liked the sound of it.

Then I became aware, that although I was still making noise, she had stopped. I wondered where my mind had been. There was emptiness and coolness.

Her hands were around my hips and stomach. I could feel them slipping on the perspiration. She tried to wipe them off on my back, but that was wet too. I wondered if the cool air coming in the window would give me pneumonia.

She pulled my hair so my head tilted back. "You're a good girl, aren't you Chris?" she said.

"I guess so." It sounded embarrassing, as I had felt as a child when told I was good. I had always hated it.

"Yes. You're a good girl. You try to pretend you're a bad girl, but you're really a very good girl."

I usually thought of myself as a bad girl pretending to be a good girl, but now this sounded absolutely true. "I don't know what I am," I said.

I could hear an argument, and car horns, and Spanish music from outside. "You're shivering," she said, and got something she put over me. Then I fell asleep.

I awoke to her hands on my body, jerking me upright.

"Take these off now," I said, extending my still-bound hands.

"Stand up," she ordered.

"But my hands—"

"Stand up." It had been so long my legs were cramped, and I had trouble balancing. "How do you feel?" she asked.

"I don't know. Weird."

She touched a nipple. "These are still erect."

"I'm cold."

She laughed. "I'm going to give you your clothing. Except your underpants. Which I'll keep." (My Victoria's Secret underpants!)

"You want me to leave?"

"Yes."

"I'm not spending the night?"

"No."

"But—"

"Don't argue with me. You'll learn it only makes things worse."

'You'll learn.' Did that mean she was planning to see me again?

"It would be a lot easier to get dressed if I could see what I was doing."

"This isn't about 'easy.'"

She handed me my shorts, then my sandals. With my hands still bound I had to sit on the floor to put them on. I could feel a slight coating of dead skin and fecal mites etc., which I was sure were stuck to the wetness between my legs. I would have liked to ask for a tissue, as after a pap smear, so my shorts wouldn't get gunky, but I was mad she was making me leave and didn't want to give her the satisfaction of knowing I was still aroused. Only when I stood to zip them up did I realize the shorts were on inside out, and I had to sit down again to put them on right.

"What about my shirt?" I asked, when the sandals were on and I was standing up.

"I'm going to undo your hands, then I'll give you your shirt, then I'll lead you into the hall."

"What about the blindfold?"

"You'll be able to take it off in the hall."

"But I want to see what you look like." She said nothing, just unhooked the restraints from my wrists. "You mean, you're not going to let me see you?"

"No."

"Why not?"

"I don't want you to."

"Why?"

"Because *I* make the rules, and *you* follow them."

Suddenly furious, I grabbed the blindfold and tried to rip it off. I saw the merest flash of light, a dark brown (black?) edge of a squarish shape – before she grabbed my hands and pushed me against the wall so hard my breath thudded out of me; less force and I would have fallen to the floor. "Try that again, and you'll never come back." She spoke softly but intensely; I felt drops of water landing on my face. "Do you understand?"

I pushed back. In my anger I was almost her equal, then it suddenly went away and, exhausted, I collapsed against the wall. I felt relaxed, empty, almost as if I had come.

I began to cry. She let go of my hands. I did not try to remove the blindfold, but let it absorb my tears.

20

Calmly, she gave me her instructions. She would open the door, I would go into the hall and spin in a circle at least ten times so that when I stopped I would not know which way I was facing. Then I could remove the blindfold and leave it draped over the banister. Assuming I did this to her satisfaction (she would be watching through the peephole to make sure I did what she said) and she heard my feet going down the stairs, she would drop my keys over the edge of banister, where they would fall to the ground floor. But if I looked up to see what she looked like, she would keep them.

"You must be *really* ugly," I said. She didn't reply.

I heard a click, then I felt a breeze. Not a fresh breeze, but one with the smell of onions and old garbage. I waited for her to kiss me, but she pushed me into the hall and shut the door.

Feeling self-conscious, in case a neighbor was watching, I rotated ten times in a rather controlled spin. Even so, it was hard to keep track of my original direction, and I was surprised when I stopped and took off the blindfold to find myself facing the stairway. I had thought I'd be facing a door – *her* door.

I looked at them all, trying to figure out which one was hers. I realized I had never tried to look in the peephole of my door (or anybody else's) from the outside, to see if you could see anything within. But of course, I would not necessarily recognize her apartment, or her, even if I were in it (though I had a kind of inner map of what it and she must look like).

Then I remembered, she had ordered me to go directly down the stairs, and not to try and figure out which was her apartment. I imagined her peeking out the hole, studying my gestures, deciding whether or not I'd crossed over the line. "Hey—" I started to say. But by what name should I address her?

I thought of keeping the blindfold, as a kind of clue. But what if she wouldn't see me again?

Did I even want to see her again?

Confused, squinting on account of the light, my shorts wet and clammy, I stumbled down the stairs. There was a clink below, a tinkling of metal as the keys bounced. Quickly, I looked up the stairwell. Did I see something move or was this merely a retinal tic?

I picked up the keys and slammed the outside door without leaving. I took a position next to the first floor banister. But no one appeared, and eventually I left.

21

Outside was a shock, like walking into sunlight after a movie. Cars were honking, streetlights glowed, several girls stood around an old-fashioned convertible, the kind that had soft red leather and wide bench seats. I kept rubbing my eyes, as if by shutting them I could find myself back inside. But no, this was the normal world, where people ate, talked, held hands in utter ignorance of what life was all about. I wanted to shake them, I wanted to see my friends, I wanted someone to come over and shove her fist into my body without asking if it was okay.

Slowly I walked up the street. There was a little Spanish restaurant at the corner with a few outdoor tables, metal enameled white, with a hole in the center for an umbrella, the surface latticed so crumbs could fall to the street. Without thinking I sat down at the only empty one. People at the other tables, beer bottles in front of them, but no food, stared at me oddly, as if there were some weird marks on my neck. Perhaps there were. I was about to get up to look in the side-view mirror of a car when the waitress walked over.

"Is it too late to eat?" I asked. "*Comida*?" I said, gesturing with my hand to my mouth.

She shook her head, then brought over someone who spoke English. "What would you like?" the man asked.

"Menu please. And a beer."

"What kind?"

I looked around. Everyone was drinking Corona. "Corona," I said. I dislike Corona, but I couldn't think of any other name.

He handed me the menu. Everything sounded good. I asked about the fried fish. "Why don't you try this?" the man pointed to something else. "It's our special."

It was also fish, but made with onions and peppers. Fried plantains came with it too. "Okay."

I hadn't realized I was hungry, but when the food came I began shoving plantains into my mouth with my hands, chewing new pieces before I'd even finished swallowing the old. It was all I could do to use a fork for the fish. It was very tasty, the way I like, though I had to be careful about the bones. Even the bread was delicious.

In my benevolence, I ordered another Corona, though it had no real taste.

I finished the plantains. Nobody ever finishes plantains. Everyone – the waitress, the man, the people at the other tables – was smiling at me. I felt happy, as if this were the first time in my life I had really tasted food.

"Would you like something else?" the man asked.

"Flan."

The flan was delicious. When I was done I ordered a second, though of course it wasn't as good.

22

I thought of calling Leslie when I got home, to surprise her about my encounter, but I didn't. Instead, I took out my vibrator. It was not to come, it was not to get excited, it was ... to remind me of something....

Far away, a drone ... a lawnmower, a prop plane, my ass in the air....

23

There was nothing at the postal box. I went every day, then twice a day, and I would have gone more often (the mere un-locking of the box brought me the ephedrine rush of anticipation) did I not worry about the guy who worked there becoming suspicious; I'd been told some people use them as drug drops. Instead I sat across the street, watching for the mail delivery, in the tiny park with its gated area for children, careful not to eye them too intently lest I become prey to a different kind of suspicion, and growing to recognize some of the others who used the mailboxes, perhaps for a similar purpose. For all I knew there were thousands – perhaps hundreds of thousands! – of such mailboxes all over the city, all rented by people leading secret lives, though if you bothered to look it was really not so secret.

Young, old, men, women, straight, gay – all seemed to be receiving more mail than me.

I invented little stories to explain why she hadn't contacted me, and replayed the language of these stories endlessly in my head: 'she lost the address,' 'she's out of town,' 'she was hit by a car,' 'she has a lover,' 'it's part of her "standard" torture routine,' 'I pulled the blindfold off too soon.' Or, worse: 'I got too wet,' 'I'm too old,' 'she doesn't like my smell.'

Sometimes I imagined she had put the ad in as a lark and hadn't expected anyone to respond, that I was the only person in the world sick enough to answer.

I consoled myself with the thought that it didn't really matter, no one had to know about it, not even my shrink.

Part of my problem, of course, was that I thought of myself as 'no one.'

Other times I imagined hordes of women had answered her ad and that, out of fairness, she was trying us all out, until she decided who was worthy of her continued attention. In my inexperience, my predictability, my over-excitement, my wetness, surely I was not.

But a voice inside me also said: what was there to be worthy of?

24

I resented leaving the house, even to go to the health club or to buy food, as this distracted me from thinking about her. Narratives of any sort repelled me, as they intruded other stories into mine. I held the phone to my ear as my friends talked, but I did not listen, nor did I confide, even in Leslie, what I had done. It was the first time in my life I had managed to keep something so big, so hidden.

When I had decided not to join the Current in Sweden, I had, in the back of my mind, a notion of joining some friends in a summer share at the beach, or renting a small house by myself for a month or two. But as I lay around time continued to pass, and the houses and shares were gone. I liked the beach, I really did. But a passive mode was spreading over me, and I was unable and did not even care to resist it.

The messages I left on her voicemail changed, from *Yearning for you* to *Still anxious to please* to *Why don't you call?* to *At least let me know why*.

25

I stopped masturbating, a kind of religious self-denial, though I told myself it was because I did not want to be swollen and numb when at last she contacted me. After several days, when this didn't work, I began masturbating constantly, partly as a form of cargo cult, but also of perverse thinking (she would only call at the very moment I did not want her, when I was too swollen to feel her touch).

The next time I tried her voicemail, a mechanical voice said the number was no longer in service.

26

Telling myself I was going to the movies, I headed east. Normally I am too impatient to walk, but now I found myself too impatient to take a taxi. I purposefully took extra-long strides, consciously pushing off with my toes to stretch my hamstrings, my right fist pounding into my left hand: "fuck, oh fuck, oh fuck..."

I soon found myself on her block. The sun beat down fero-
ciously, so intense that it was not just heat, but almost a physical
presence. I took refuge at a little deli, where I bought an iced
cappuccino that was not half bad. As hot as it was, under the
awning it was cool, almost chilled, so I moved back into the sun.
I leaned against a car and the metal burned my ass through
my shorts. After the coffee was gone, I continued to suck the
undissolved coffee-flavored sugar crystals from the bottom of
the cup. Just being on her block, with the shadows of cars and
trees so sharp they looked surreal, I was happier than I had
been in days.

It was not the first time I had stood outside a building waiting
for someone to appear, and I was not unhappy to be doing so
again, for it reminded me of other times of happiness – or, rather,
moments when I had thought happiness might appear.

The smart people were inside, though someone was working
on the engine of a car.

A blond but Spanish-looking woman walked out of the
building, with a short burly guy whose hair curled out of his tee-
shirt. This could not be her – she was short and stocky, and
young Elvis was thin and tall. Nor was she (I prayed!) this skinny
bleached blonde who seemed in her upper teens, but was
probably almost 30, heading towards the park with a little girl.
Nor that women with monstrous tits, nor the one with the
obnoxious kids, nor was she, of course, a man carrying two
dark-green plastic bags.

I joined the man who was using water from a hydrant to
wash his car, cupping the water in my palms and releasing it
over my head. The sun warmed it almost immediately. I nodded

at the man, but he looked away, as if I were an undercover cop or a journalist working on a drug story. Was this why no one tried to sell me anything? I smelled grilled hamburger. Out of the air floated the occasional sentence, clearly audible yet spoken so softly it was almost a whisper. I could hear the clacking of silverware on tables. I used to live in a neighborhood like this, a real neighborhood with real people who had children at normal ages. A better neighborhood, really, than where I lived now. People who sat on the steps at night, people whose cars shared music with you, people who sweated as they made love in a room without air-conditioning, people who got pregnant without the aid of hormones and an army of doctors, people with dogs and cats and parakeets and gold fish in rooms stuffed with tacky furniture and calendars on the walls.

Without planning, utterly forgetting that I was violating our agreement (which gave her the "right" – obligation? – never to see me again (was that why I was doing it?)) I crossed the street and entered her building.

I walked to the top floor and put my ear to the door I thought she was in (SW). I didn't hear anything. I pressed the buzzer and then, when that didn't work, banged on the door.

When nobody answered I tried the door diagonally opposite (NE). "Yeah?" a man's voice shouted.

I turned back to SW, then remembered that before taking the blindfold off I had thought it was SE, because the door seemed to be on the left side, but then I remembered bumping my right arm against the wall, so maybe it was SW after all (unless I was facing the other way and it was NE), but it couldn't be NE because of the man. Unless . . . . (I decided not to follow this thought). I got so confused I could no longer remember what I had thought with my eyes shut, only that when I opened them what I saw was a surprise. I was not sure if the impulse I felt now (SE) was a "real" impulse or a kind of averaging of the memories of other impulses. I walked to the door and moved my hands a few centimeters over the surface, as if to sense hidden sources of energy. My hands trembled. I listened. Perhaps I heard something. Chinese? I knocked.

I was so high (adrenaline? caffeine? sugar? serotonin?) my brain danced, my skin emanated odors. Lights glowed, wavered, rainbows were around them. My feet, in their sandals, were wet. The Chinese stopped. My feet smelled, there was music.

I almost tripped as the door was opened, by a man, but not Chinese. "Sorry," I said. I pointed next door, but he was shouting to a woman inside, in a language I did not understand, like Spanish but also like German. She came to the door carrying a frying pan.

She shouted at me in a language that sounded neither like German nor Spanish (nor Chinese). Exaggeratedly I shrugged my shoulders, raised my palms, started backing away (my hands now clasped together before my face as if I were from India) as she and the man began arguing.

Was I crazy or was the woman suddenly speaking English? Her neighbors, she said, had gone away for the summer.

"Thank you, thank you," I repeated, hands still in prayer position.

The woman smiled, the man shut the door.

27

You have broken your word. By all rights I should not see you again. However, I will offer a reprieve, in the form of a penance.... I was to appear at a certain East Village bar Friday at midnight, dressed in black miniskirt, heels, fishnet stockings, a black bra under an open black lace top embroidered with the words "S E X S L A V E." No underpants. Bright red lipstick. As a sign of my contrition I could drink only water, and I had to dance/go home, etc. with anyone who asked. If I brought a friend, or even an accomplice to keep an eye on me from a distance, I would never hear from her again.

It was Wednesday.

How had she known I had broken my word? Unless she was the blond Spanish woman after all? Or the one with the obnoxious kids. More likely the woman with the frying pan had told her of a visitor. (But she said her neighbors had gone away for the summer. (Unless she was the woman with the frying pan....))

Excited and intrigued, I reread the note.

Long before punk, or androgyny, or Drag Kings, I had foresworn skirts and heels, initially from principle, then by habit, so that I no longer know how to wear them. Or rather, for me, skirts and heels *were* drag. I had never felt like I belonged in them, though photos of me dressed in such fashion attest to the apparent normalcy of my appearance. I could never figure out what to do with my hands, and because I hated banging my legs together and hurting them, my knees always angled out-wards, which made me look wobbly and unconvincing in heels, not that (as I discovered) I could any longer fit into mine, and the Current's were too large.

I wasted $120 on a pair, amusing the salesperson greatly with my attempts to walk in them.

28

The skirt, the bra, the halter top, the stockings, lay on a chair next to the bed. The gel, mascara, foundation, eyeliner, were on the shelf near the sink. The weather, which had been dreary all day, matched my mood. In the natural light, where I had had to squint to see myself, my face had looked silvery, my figure mysterious, almost like a ghost. When I turned on the light, I no longer possessed the poignancy of the half-visible, but looked sickly and yellow. Funny pyramids of shadow appeared by my nose and under my lip. There were lines I did not remember, which, now that I had brought them into consciousness, I would surely continue to see. My face was heavier than I remembered, and the silver glints in my hair seemed gray.

My skin did not glow. Perhaps it never had. My nose seemed thicker.

I held out my arms. Skin still firm, thanks to the health club, no skin hanging down. There were some black spots – hopefully freckles, but maybe moles! Were they new or had they been there my whole life? I could not remember.

I took off my pants. My thighs seemed heavy, my knees scarred. Even in the natural light, I could see the round outline of my stomach.

I put on water for the bath, and found some old bath oil the Current had brought back from France. I hate France. The oil had not been used in some time, and I had trouble opening the bottle.

My hamstrings were tight, and I slowly bent down from the waist, letting my hands touch the floor, to stretch them. I shut my eyes and smelled the oil and waited to see if tears would pour out of them. They did not.

When I opened my eyes, I saw, upside-down in the mirror, the round ass and thick thighs of a middle-aged woman. *Who's that*? I thought, for a second.

I pounded my hand on the wall. Looking at myself in the mirror the normal way, I tried to see myself as I had in the morning. But it was hard to get the image of that upside-down ass out of my mind.

How dare I worry about what anyone else's ass looks like? I thought. But I did.

29

After the bath I put on the make-up. I had not done this in some time, and I had to wash the eyeliner off repeatedly before I got it right.

I sat by the window. The rain had at least stopped; street-lights and headlights were reflected in the already drying puddles. The men had re-emerged, on their way to their perfect silent exchanges. I envied them their simplicity, their candor, their perfect understanding of their bodies, the way they separated the Realm of the Body from the Realm of the Mind, thereby becoming Rulers of both.

We attack men for this, of course. Who does not attempt to

destroy what one cannot have?

But why could we not have it? Because men were simple, women complex? Because our genitals were curved, ridged, circled on themselves, like a mountain chain, so you could not say precisely where one lip stopped and another began? Because inside gradually became outside, and there was no dividing line? Because our veins fell out of our bodies, ugly and swollen, after giving birth, rather than staying inside where they belonged? Because our wet leaked out rather than came in spurts? Because it evaporated rather than left dried patches on sheets? Because we came not definitively but in waves, and sometimes it was impossible to say "how often" or even if "at all"? Because sometimes it was better to use a vibrator over underpants or sheet or even comforter, rather than touch ourselves directly? Because ... because ... because ....

30

I sat at the bar with a glass of water, which I pretended was vodka, gazing at the relatively tame scenarios of humiliation and lust presented by the tv monitors above the bar.

Although the content of the videos was not 'politically correct,' the nature of the participants, women of properly varying colors and shapes and sizes and ages, demonstrated the politically correct nature of our desires.

It had been awhile since more banal scenarios could reasonably be expected to arouse us.

I stared at the women entering the bar. Since I did not know what she looked like, the only way I would know for sure it was her was by the look of recognition in her eyes as she spotted me.

Of course she could already be there, seeing if I was obeying her orders, before announcing her presence.

I felt a kind of pity for her, in that I was certain I would not be attracted to her. I am not attracted to most people. I practiced forming a face that would conceal my disappointment. Perhaps it would be better if she did not come, so I could keep the memory of our night intact. I would feel like a fool, of course, for going to all this trouble, but there are worse things than being a fool.

Luckily, my concern about *my* appearance, anxiety-provoking as it was, took away from my concern about *her* appearance.

It is possible, of course, that the memory of what I had let her do to me would make her seem, in a perverse way, attractive.

But time passed, and I saw no sign of recognition in anyone's eyes, or even acknowledgment. Eyes grazed by me without stopping, as women headed for the dance floor or the down-stairs bar as if I were transparent or invisible, instead of the absurd transvestite I was.

I could not understand why I was not happy like everybody else, in some simple relationship as they were, where I felt like going out Saturday night and dancing with the person I lived with.

I could understand going out with someone I lived with, and I could understand dancing, but not the two concepts together.

Out of habit, not knowing what to do with my hands, I found myself quickly swallowing glass after glass of water, though I was not thirsty and in the metaphysical sense it was absurd to pay $3 for something that came out of the tap for free. But of course the bottling was not free, or the shipping, and my purchases, in their own small way, contributed to the smooth functioning of the economic system. Nonetheless it annoyed me. And it annoyed me that it annoyed me, because this was the voice of my father, arguing that bottled water was just a con for restaurants to make money off all those reformed alkies who no longer ordered wine. He said this every time I ordered bottled water in a restaurant, and I ordered it every time I was with him – if only to annoy him. Reflexively I'd argue how the water was of better quality, and reflexively he'd argue how it all came out of a tap.

(How happy he was when Perrier was found to be contaminated! How I triumphed when Giuliani announced the pipes of New York were leaching lead!)

When the water was gone I'd suck on the lime, then wait for some ice to melt and drink a little more. And so the time passed.

I put off going to the john, in case I was in the bathroom when she arrived and we missed each other. But the line was getting longer, so finally I joined it. I leaned against the wall as I usually did, then realized how ridiculous this looked in skirt and heels and straightened up. But I immediately forgot, and found myself slouching again.

I was conscious of my thighs lightly sticking to each other under my skirt. This seemed slightly obscene, and appropriate that it should be hidden.

The consciousness of thighs – was that why women wore skirts? I was also unduly conscious of my ass.

There was no toilet paper in the holder of the stall, but a roll was on the floor. Normally I would not use this. I bent down to pick it up, but it was wet. "Ughhhhh," I heard myself say as it fell from my hand.

I pushed opened the stall door with my knee and, the points

of my heels catching on the tiles, walked in tiny steps like a Chinese woman to the sink. I turned on the faucet with my left hand and stuck my right under the water. When it had gotten thoroughly soaked, I used it to push the bar of soap into the sink. After the water dissolved the top layer, I washed my hands. Then I dried them. Then I washed them again. It would have been embarrassing – or perhaps impossible – to do this had anyone else been in the bathroom. When I was done, I grabbed a handful of the brown paper towels that sat piled on a chair by the sink and hobbled back into the stall.

I covered the toilet seat with paper towels, then I sat down. The towels were rough and not very supple, refusing to mold themselves to the little curves and inlets of my body after I'd peed. Toilet paper in foreign countries was often like this, and I often wondered how people could stand it. Despite the amount of time I had spent thinking about this over the years, I had never discussed this problem with anyone. No one ever talked about what happened to the little drops toilet paper and towels did not pick up, and how our tongues, later in the evening, traversing these same places, would dissolve the dried-up residue in our saliva.

After leaving the bathroom, I went to the dance area, trying to accustom my eyes to the dark.

On a tiny stage, at the end of the room, a tall black girl with a shaved head danced. Her eyes were shut and she seemed oblivious of her audience. Her nipples were covered with glitter, and she wore a skirt that seemed to be made of two foot-long strands of paper. Near her was a white girl, who would occasionally leave the stage and mingle with the customers. Her hands were bound together with chains, and she wore a black leather bra and G-string.

I did not find this sexy, but presumably other people did.

Over the dance floor was a strobe, which, via some homeo-pathic function, calmed rather than excited me, as if the extremely fast alternations of light and dark were less a visual mimicking than an external embodiment of the pounding in my chest and my quick shallow breaths.

The more the strobe flashed the calmer I grew, and the further away the music and people.

"You wanna dance?" I heard someone say.

A tall woman with short black hair, wearing a black leather vest over a long white shirt, and blue jeans, was talking to me. She wore a little red AIDS ribbon pinned to her vest.

My heart sank as I said "yes."

She pushed through the dancers to create a space for us. Mostly I moved my arms, in an interpretation of the last dance I had truly learned (the frug), shifting my weight from one foot to the other to create the impression of mobility, as I could not move easily in my heels. It was so hard to be a real girl.

Normally, after ten minutes or so, when the endorphins kicked in, I would start to enjoy myself and dance a little better – or, maybe, because I was enjoying myself, I would *feel* I was dancing better.

It did not happen now, however, partly because of the shoes, partly because of my self-consciousness about my dress, but mostly because I don't dance well with someone I don't want to have sex with.

With my eyes open I was not attracted to her, but as I leaned against her the memory of the things we had done aroused me and made me wet – perhaps *especially* because I was not attracted to her, and would not be able to do such things with her again.

She stuck her hand under my skirt and slid it up my stockings. The note had said I had to let people do what they wanted, so I let her. She squeezed my thighs. Then she moved her hands further up. "No panties," she said. The song changed. I tried to move my legs together, so nobody would see, but she held them apart with her arms. She began pulling my pubic hairs. I pretended I was a young girl – a small-town slut – being picked up by a man in some small town honky-tonk bar. He would buy me drinks and take me home, and we would pretend it happened because I was drunk – and I *would* be drunk, but that would not be why it had happened.

I shut my eyes, not so I would pretend it was not happening – because its happening was what was arousing me – but so that it would be more like a fantasy than a real event. I told myself we were so blocked in by other people it would be almost impossible for anyone to figure out what she was doing.

One hand held my butt; the other tried to enter me, a finger or two anyway, from behind. Due to the angle she had trouble doing this. I pushed my ass out slightly to help, but it didn't.

As she moved her right hand back toward the front I had to move my body away from hers to make space for her hand. I leaned against her, so her arm was hidden, almost trapped by my body. But she managed to maneuver enough to get one finger, then another, inside me, in the ordinary place.

"Box 392," I said, but she seemed not to notice, even when I repeated it a bit more loudly.

At the end of the song she pulled her fingers out of me. "I've got to go to the bathroom," she said. I started to follow her off the dance floor. But she said: "Wait here. I'll be right back."

Almost immediately, a slightly overweight but attractive black woman asked me to dance. "You seem to be having a good time," she said.

"I like to dance," I blushed. She chuckled, then moved her hand up my skirt to my thigh, as the first woman had done.

"What happened to your friend?" she asked.

"I don't know."

"Should I go look for her?"

By now her fingers were almost where the other woman's had been. "Not really," I breathed.

"You seemed such good friends," she said, reproachfully.

"I never saw her before."

"Really?" Her fingers were now inside me.

I was leaning on her hand, pressing it more inside me. A thin sheen of perspiration seemed to cover my whole body. If she had brought me up to the little stage to display me, I would have let her.

I shut my eyes, but her voice was not familiar either. Her breasts were comfortable, but perhaps too large. The pounding music made it seem like a music video, a dream.

The voice was not familiar. The breasts were not familiar. This I knew. But when I tried to remember what Box's were like, I couldn't.

"*Slut*." At least I think that's what I heard as she withdrew her hand and pushed me upright. Or was it something else, like "wait" or "shit," or did she say nothing at all? I felt dazed. The strobe flickered as she walked away.

I stood in the center of the floor, self-conscious and alone. When I looked up, I saw the black woman and the woman with short black hair standing together by the bar. They fell silent as I walked past them, then burst out laughing. This laughter, or my hallucination of this laughter, stayed with me throughout the night, co-existing oddly with the apparently contradictory notion that I was invisible.

No one else came over to me. I stayed until 4, when last call was announced, when the truly desperate teamed up for the night. I was truly desperate, but no one approached me, and I had to go home alone.

31

I had not eaten. The deli had no healthy, plain yogurt, only the kind with lots of artificial-tasting jam in the bottom. Still in the store, waiting to pay, I ripped off the top of a papaya one and began spooning it into my mouth. But the color and smell reminded me of vomit. I left it uneaten, for the homeless, on top of a large aluminum garbage can outside the store.

I passed Day-Glo Pizza, with its counter of blazing lavender formica. Too hungry to wait for the oven, I shoved a cold Sicilian slice in my mouth. The mozzarella stretched like gum; I was unable to bite through it. I swallowed, but as I had half-consciously feared (in that tiny part of a second between intent and action), the cheese just stretched in an even longer string from the plate to my esophagus.

I grabbed a handful of napkins from the metal stand and tried to spit out the cheese, but a piece stuck in my throat.

As if I were not choking, life went on around me, slowly, slowly, under the absurdly bright light, as if we were in a film, a film with vivid (albeit stereotypical) "characters" – blacks in their early twenties, a white hetero couple, young dykettes in a corner. There was even a soundtrack, a song I did not recognize, like most of the songs of the past fifteen years; in all honesty, could I even distinguish grunge from heavy metal? Soon I would stumble over to someone – the black guys – and they would save my life. Or maybe they wouldn't. But they would try.

I trusted them to do that, I realized, more than the white people who were there.

Was I breathing? I couldn't tell. I opened my mouth, stuck in my hand, and began to yank out, like a fishing reel unwinding, the strands of chewed-up cheese and bread out of my throat. It took awhile, but the cheese grew so thin it finally snapped.

I went over to the garbage bin, pushed open the gray plastic door, and dumped out the contents of my fist. I was desperate for water, but I could not stay there, and when I saw a woman and her dog getting out of a cab I ran into it, even though the girl half of a hetero couple had started to enter from the other side. Ignoring her, I lay my head back against the seat. Soon she and her boyfriend were cursing at me. Normally I would have cursed back, but for various reasons (fear of vomiting, IBS, heart attack) I was scared to move my lips.

They got in the cab with me. The cab driver motioned me to leave, but of course, he did not speak English and I pretended not to understand him. I shut my eyes. He gave up and headed for the address they gave him. At first the girl and her boyfriend tried to insult me, talking about me as if I weren't there, but as I showed no sign of response their hearts went out of it and they fell silent. When they left the cab, I gave the driver my address, and after some procrastination he drove me home.

32

"You're a good girl, Chris," she wrote. *"I hear you were wonderful at the bar. See you Saturday at the usual place and time...."*

What did she mean she 'heard' I was 'wonderful?' Was that a ruse, or had she really not been at the club? Had it been a friend of hers who had danced with me? Had she told someone – maybe a group of people – about me? Was there some organization of women like her, who exchanged information about their 'slaves'? Was there a shadow government in the city of owners and slaves, like the Mafia but oriented toward sex rather than money, that I had unknowingly become part of, with its own customs, manners, and mode of dress, its laws that brooked no appeal?

It was frightening, of course, but compelling. Writers are inevitably drawn toward narrative, no matter how repugnant.

33

For my second visit the blindfold was again on the floor (though without a note), and on her orders I again walked backwards down the stairs.

As I undressed she said: "In the future it is unnecessary for me to attend to the preliminaries. You can put on the blindfold yourself, walk down the stairs, etc., until I summon you. Once inside the apartment, you will immediately strip and wait patiently for further instructions. Do not always expect me to be attentive to your every movement. Sometimes you will be kept waiting.

Do not sit, squat, or do anything else without permission, not just when you first enter, but the entire time you are with me."

I was lying over the couch, my hands bound together by the same soft straps, my ass bare, the short skirt she had ordered me to wear hiked up around my hips.

She was running the head of the whip casually up and down my crack as she discussed the beauties and imperfections of my body. "How soft, how round and white, so very welcoming. Very clean. Very soft. Very pliant." She whacked me a little. "A little red maybe now. But very soft. *Very* welcoming." She touched me. "*Very* wet. Very gushing. Very gooey. Very smelly." She brought my hand up to me.

"I'm not smelly," I said. But I wasn't sure. Maybe I was losing my mind. Maybe this was what people meant by 'smell.' Maybe what I had always thought was smelly wasn't to anybody else. Maybe I was color-blind about smell.

"Very wet. Very warm. Very smelly." She bent down, kissed me, then bit me.

"*Ow*," I said.

"Soft. Warm. Smelly. Isn't it?" Pause. Whack. "Isn't it?"

"Yes."

"Yes *what*?" Whack.

"Very smelly."

"So soft. So white." Whack. "So welcoming. You love me to do this, don't you, Chris?"

"Yes."

"And why do you love it?"

I had thought much about this, to no avail. "I don't know."

Whack. "Of course you do."

"*Ow*. I don't. I *don't*."

Whack. "Why, Chris?"

"Because my parents didn't spank me?"

Whack.

"Because I want to be punished for sleeping with women?"

Whack.

"Because if you make the decisions I don't have to feel guilty?"

Whack.

"Because I'm a sick fuck?"

Whack.

"Because I love you?"

Whack.

"Because I don't know what love is?"

Whack. Whack. Whack.

"I don't know. I don't know, I don't know." I began to sob.

When I was done she took me down the hall and placed me on a bed. I lay face up, with my arms tied apart.

Very gently she put her lips on mine, without moving. We lay there with them touching a long time, and then, very slowly, I opened my mouth and extended my tongue, as if we were on a first date. I touched her upper lip lightly a long time, then the lower, then I moved my tongue inside to touch her teeth. I licked the front of her upper teeth, then the lower, then I lightly licked her gums. I forced open the teeth and slipped my tongue inside until I touched, just lightly, her tongue. But this was not about kissing, it was about licking. I licked behind her lower teeth, then up to her palette, then I tried to tickle the top of her throat. I loved her so much I started to cry, but not from pain.

"You're mine," she almost whispered, "you'd do anything for me, wouldn't you?"

"Yes," I whispered back.

She licked my tears. I felt as if I loved her. I felt she loved me, though I knew she wouldn't say it.

"Shall we make a contract, Chris?"

"What?"

"A contract. I want you to be totally available to me." A warm wave went through me. "Isn't that what you want?"

"Yes," I said.

"I thought so. I think this has the possibility of becoming a good relationship, don't you?"

"I thought it already was."

"Oh Chris." She sounded sad. "How much you have to learn. But you're a good student, aren't you?" With no preparation, she jammed her finger in my rectum.

"Ow. God. That *really* hurts. Ow. Please stop." For she was pushing it in and out very quickly. It was very dry.

"Would you like some lubrication?" she asked.

"Yes."

"Yes, *please*."

"Yes, *please*," I repeated.

"Luckily, we've got a friend." She left the bed. "Charlie. Oh, Charlie."

Charlie! A man was there – a friend? lover? – watching me, laughing at me, a man who had seen me spanked, seen her put her finger in my rectum, heard me cry, tell her I loved her. And I couldn't move. I tried to get away, but I couldn't move. The straps cut into my wrists, but I could not get free.

Something jumped on the bed. There was bouncing, panting. Fur tickled me.

"Meet Charlie," she said.

Charlie barked. Charlie was a dog.

At first I was grateful it wasn't a human being – someone who could tell on me.

Then I felt even worse.

"No!" I shouted. "You can't do this. It's not fair." For Charlie was trying to lick my face. I could smell his breath. I kept turning my head back and forth. His saliva landed on me. He moved down the bed and I began kicking at him.

"Get down, Charlie," she ordered. "*Charlie.*"

Charlie jumped off the bed. I could hear him panting by my ear.

"I thought you wanted lubrication."

"That's not what I meant."

"You can sometimes get what you want, Chris, but you can't expect to get it exactly the way you want it. Now are you going to let Charlie lick you?"

"I don't know."

She slapped my stomach, hard. It didn't feel the least erotic.

"Ow."

She slapped me again. "Are you?"

I nodded, and Charlie got back on the bed. I was able to bear his licking my stomach, but when he moved elsewhere I again started kicking. But she was holding my legs down. "No," I heard myself screaming. "I can't. Stop. Please. Don't." But Charlie was continuing. "I can't. Really. Please. Red. Red. *Red.*"

She stopped. Save for Charlie's panting, it was silent.

I was crying – but a different kind of crying than before. She didn't say anything. I heard nothing, not even the sound of her breath. For all I knew she had left the room. But Charlie was still there, snuffling at my feet.

"I didn't think it would be like this," I said. "I don't think I can take it." She didn't say anything. "You better untie me and let me go home," I said.

"If that's what you want."

She undid my arms, both from the bed and each other. I was surprised. I had expected her to argue with me. Or even to ignore my request.

I brought my arms to my side and hugged myself. I was shivering.

"Get under the sheet," she said.

I lifted myself up so she could get the sheet out from under me. Then she covered me with a blanket.

We were silent a long time. I was crying. "I've never done this before."

"I know."

"I mean, with *anyone*. I've done some stuff. But not this."

"Maybe you can't handle it."

"I don't think so. I'd like to, but I can't."

"If you can't, you can't." She put her hand on my neck. A warm wave rushed through me. I would lose this if I left.

"Aren't you going to argue with me?" I finally asked.

"No."

"Maybe we could just have a normal relationship," I said. "I mean, I know it wouldn't be the same, but...." She laughed. "Well, I guess that's not what this is about."

"No...."

She was stroking my neck. I felt happy again. I moved my head closer to her leg, and I rested it on her. I began to lick her leg. I lay there drooling – not so different from Charlie, when you think about it.

Again, I heard voices from other apartments, music, shouts from the street. I remembered these sounds from when I was younger and would spend a night with anyone who asked. I was so poor then I ate yogurt for lunch every single day, and I would go to the trouble to buy TDF vouchers to save a dollar fifty when I went to off-off-Broadway plays.

I would hardly go out of my way to save twenty dollars now, but could I say I was any happier?

"I like the East Village," I said. "I never exactly lived here, but I've always liked sleeping with people who lived here. It's much... *realer* than... the upper West Side." With her stroking me, and the music, and my crying, it felt very familial, like I had lived there a long time with her.

"You mean the West *Village*, don't you?"

"Why do you say that?" I asked. "That's not where I live."

"No?"

Charlie snorted.

What had she meant by bringing Charlie into the room? Was Charlie supposed to fuck me, or only lick me?

I heard the words – 'only lick me' – and a deep wave of shame went through me. But the wave was followed by warmth.

I crawled into her arms and buried my head in her breasts. "It's okay if Charlie just licks me," I whispered.

She was rubbing my head. "You mean, you *want* Charlie to lick you?"

"*No!* But if you really want me to, I'm willing to do it. If—"

"If it means continuing our relationship?"

"Yes."

"But our relationship isn't about Charlie, Chris. It's about you obeying me. Absolutely and completely, doing what I tell you, *not* because you're turned on by the idea, but because I tell you to do it."

"I know." I hated the whine in my voice.

"You don't act like you know. You're very willful, Chris. You act like you're running this show. But you're not."

Suddenly it sounded boring, like my parents. "Okay, okay." I was no longer turned on. I rolled over into the pillows.

She pulled them away. "I want you to go home and think this over. If you're really willing to be in this kind of relationship. Maybe you're not."

"How long do I have to think about it?"

"As long as you want."

"Oh." A deadline would be easier.

"And if I decide I want to?"

"You'll let me know."

"But your voice mail is disconnected."

"I have a postal box, like you."

She started to pull away. I tried to hold her, but she said "stop." I stopped.

"You know," I said, waving my free hands at the blindfold, "I could have ripped this off at any time."

"I knew you wouldn't," she said. "You really *are* a good girl."

She patted me, like she might have Charlie. We were silent a moment. I thought of ripping the blindfold off and surprising her and myself. But I did not.

"Stand up," she said. "We'll get you your clothes."

I gave her my hand and she led me to the living room. Without my hands tied it was easier to put on my clothes.

"I don't know your name," I told her. "What should I call you?"

"Do I know *your* name, 'Chris?'" she asked.

34

Without thinking, I found myself in front of The Bar. Girls in their black shorts, their white shirts, their tattoos and navel rings, stood outside, flirting with each other. I would have leaned against the cars with them, drinking beer and smoking, but I was afraid someone would recognize me. A person like me is never supposed to be alone. But I only felt like myself when I was alone. Gay men passed by, earrings in their ears, heads shaved in odd patterns, nipple rings in their tits, even weirder than the chicks.

I went inside only to reassure myself nobody was there so I could go home and sleep and not torture myself that I was missing something.

If someone had come up to me and said "come suck my dick – my beautiful latex cock," I would have, but they didn't.

I left after a few minutes. What was going on inside my mind was more interesting than what was going on inside the bar.

Fuck the cab, I walked home. It was one of those humid nights, all the world was out, men and women, men and men, women and women, arms around each other as if they liked each other, pretending to laugh, eating Haagen-Dazs ice cream bars, walking their dogs, buying *The New York Times*.

They hated each other, but they didn't know it. Only I knew it.

Restless and hyped, I walked past my building to the pier. The cops had put up a gate to keep people off it, but someone had broken the metal and folded it back. I scratched my arm slipping through the gate. You had to be careful walking; there were holes in the boards of the pier through which you could see the river, or, rather, flecks of light the river was reflecting. On the upper East Side the holes would have been surrounded by sawhorses, but not here. Yet you never heard about alkies or druggies falling in. Or maybe nobody cared if they disappeared.

You could hear the water swishing below, against the wooden pilings.

Men were cruising, indifferent to the rotting boards, the concrete barriers, me watching. I knew if I looked, I could see disgusting things. Women never cruised here, or anywhere, we were so boring.

I wondered what it would be like to be fucked in the butt, here in the moonlight.

If you walked to the end of the pier, where your view was no longer blocked by another pier a few blocks south, you could see the Statue of Liberty. The Current and I had come here once, after making love for many hours, and sat on the concrete barrier with our arms around each other. I could play the scene in my head, hear the music in the background.

The poignancy had gone. But a movie of it might have made me cry.

2.
The Letters

35

You realize, of course, I have another life.

In this other life I am not a sex slave, a pathetic middle-aged being who lives for random moments of intensity, but a writer, not famous exactly, but not unknown either. I have won prizes, I have taught, I have written reviews and been jealous of my peers.

Style is my strong point; I lack imagination. I read as I wish to be read, like a fundamentalist reads the Bible, literally, stupidly, convinced that each narrative event, whether recounted in the first or third person, whether plausible or impossible, has been personally experienced by its author.

I have friends, some distant relatives (my family being on the whole averse to propagation – you'd understand if you met them), objects and possessions, the standard detritus of a certain kind of American life. I go to movies, watch tv, work out, ski cross-country and scuba dive in warm water. I have a moderate but not inordinate interest in good food, nice restaurants, and interior design. I have been to Europe and the Caribbean many times, to the Middle East, to South America, to Asia. I subscribe to a variety of magazines, some literary, some political, some "lifestyle-oriented." I live with a feline and a human, as I have done (intermittently with humans, consistently with a feline) for years.

None of this is unusual or interesting, except perhaps the fact that I spend much of my time gambling (an activity more commonly known as "investing"), the adrenal stimulation from which a former shrink believed I was addicted to. Perhaps. I have always enjoyed games, both of the physical and mental kind, which have the advantage of being (unlike other forms of relations between people), thanks to their boundaries and other artificial qualities, utterly capable of resolution, unambiguously revelatory of winners and losers. And of all games "investing" is the oldest, the biggest, the most complex, the most demeaning or augmenting to the ego, the most prone to an infinity of strategies and tactics, the most predictably unpredictable, the most dismissive of "common sense," the most subject to the vicissitudes of "fate" or (if you prefer) "luck" – a.k.a. "climate" or "weather" or "war" or "currency fluctuations" or "fiscal policy…." etc.

I augment this income with that which I get from writing.

I am also chronically exhausted, not with some specific ailment (though who knows?), but a fatigue that has been with me my entire life. In regards to this I am a hero – a modest, silent hero, the way the men outside my window are. I go about my duties to my friends, family, career, leisure, possessions, cat, Current, and money as if there were nothing odd about this, as if I were the person meant to be doing such things, and though I often complain (albeit amusingly – so I am told), I never address the real complaint: which is that there is someone else living my life who does not enjoy it as much as I am told I should.

I was at the moment working on a novel that had been giving me much trouble. It was about a love affair which had caused me "heartbreak" (melodramatic, yes, but that's the only word that fits), turned some of my hairs gray, made me feel middle-aged – which is to say, *old*. This was not the Current, of course, but someone who shall here go nameless. Sometimes I still dreamed of her, and in that other world, our relationship – if it did not exactly "progress" – had its high points. I read a section from it July 3 on "Counting Sheep," the weekly program of a college radio station:

There are many urges, of course, in the human heart: love, hatred, jealousy, anxiety, the urge to triumph and, when one does not, the urge to appear to do so, which we know as pride. But of the many urges of the human heart, perhaps the one least acknowledged & understood is that of self-abasement. I will tell you what happened to me one time, when I was younger and unknowing in the ways of love. I had seen a young woman at a party whom I found myself attracted to, but she was more than fifteen years younger than me, and, finding myself over-conscious of this disparity, I told myself I would not pay attention to her. She was just out of college, trying to make her way in the downtown art scene, and as she chattered with her friends, some of whom were still in school, others of whom had just graduated, the way they talked about 'the world' and 'the art scene,' with its fake cynicism revealing a touchingly concealed naivete, confirmed my earlier decision not to distract her with my old world cynicism. Nonetheless, her eyes caught mine from time to time, and I half-consciously wondered if perhaps it was my very jadedness which attracted her.

About this jadedness I have two opinions. Almost surely it is justified, the things experience had taught me had been taught me for a reason, what was the point of age if not to confer wisdom? On the other hand, if, as Heraclitus has shown, each day, each minute, each second is utterly unique and unreduplicable – perhaps, just perhaps, these lessons are in fact false and misleading – rationalizations we cowards use to conceal from ourselves the utter meaninglessness, pointlessness, etcetera of life. That night, due to the youthfulness of the girl, and perhaps the soft summer air, I more than half-hoped my 'perhaps' was the correct alternative, even though this would confirm the very uselessness, irrelevancy, even vanity of my experience. For in my more altruistic moments, I told myself the relevancy of my life didn't matter – not just in the grand scheme, of course – but perhaps even to myself. Normally I was totally caught up in the frivolousness of my everyday existence – less frivolous, perhaps, than most people's, but still, in the context of the eternal, vain and superficial – but every once in a while the tedium and repetitiveness of all this would astonish me – as it were – afresh, and I would look at myself as I looked at other people, with amazement at my narcissistic egocentrism. What was I, after all, but a leaf? a bacterium in the sand of time? Could I honestly pretend that my life was significant or interesting – even to myself! – I who watched sports on television every chance I got? Obviously not. And if it was not interesting to me, why should it be interesting to other people, even as a subject of conversation, even though the amusing, self-deprecating (if I may say so myself!) mode in which I invariably spoke about it to other people – so that their laughter would absolve, as it were, my ephemera of its more negative connotations – was as far removed from the earnest, self-pitying, replete-with-significance demeanor which others brought to any discussion of their lives....

36

During a short break the producer, while playing an avant-garde musical composition so repetitious it could be interrupted at any time with perhaps not even the composer any the wiser, provided me with the coke and Perrier I had requested. Then, after a brief Q & A during which she demonstrated an almost frightening awareness of my entire *oeuvre*, she shut off the overhead lights and opened up the phone lines. In the dark, with only the glow of the knobs, the CD player and turntable, the two mikes, the questions seemed to come not from other people but the hidden parts of my own soul.

"How autobiographical is your work?" the first caller asked.

"About the same as Philip Roth."

"Is there anything you like as well as sex?"

"Sports talk radio."

"Do you think gayness is genetic?"

"For most people, yes. It's linked to the gene that causes faggots to like musicals."

Next.

"What do you think about that area in the hypothalamus that's smaller in gay men than in straight?"

"I think that if gay men's were *bigger* than straights' they wouldn't have been nearly as pissed. But the question I'm *really* interested in is, 'is a dyke's larger or smaller than a gay man's?'"

Next.

From a woman: "It sounds like an offensive book and I don't think anybody should read it."

"You're entitled to your opinion, of course, no matter how stupid it is."

After the show I acceded to the request of the producer (a graduate student in the School of Arts), to have a beer and something to eat at a nearby college-type bar – a repast paid for (as she assured me) out of the radio station's budget, during which she plied me with a lengthy series of questions concerning the writing process and my life. She seemed unduly astonished – and a bit disappointed – to hear that I lived with someone who was almost my own age. I could tell she was interested in me, but no doubt because of shyness, she refused to conform to the internal rules I have developed concerning who I will and will not have sex with: i.e., if I am seriously attracted to someone I don't mind making a pass at them, but in cases of equivocal attraction, or extreme dichotomies of age, income, achievement, or degree of physical attraction, it is up to others to make their intentions clear. Perhaps because she was young, and had not yet come to realize how easy it is for someone of that age to achieve their objectives, she did not, and so I went home alone, wondering all the while as to whether by any chance Box had been listening to the radio station and recognized my voice.

37

I had difficulty working the next few days, going so far as to actually fall asleep at the computer. I did not need my shrink (to whom I was uncharacteristically silent concerning my adventures) to tell me I was avoiding something. Eventually, after much internal debate as to style and content, including an exceedingly painstaking effort to evoke the appearance of spontaneity (lots of parentheses and dashes) I wrote:

Friday

Dear Box 392,

   Yeah. Yes. Of course. How could it be otherwise?
   I 'love you' (of course).
   I'm petrified (of course).
   A contract is on both sides, right? so here's my part: you've GOT to leave 'my life' out of this!!! By 'my life' I mean respecting my anonymity – even if you find out who I am – and you can't do anything that will impact on my relationship with the Current (any more than this obviously will, that is!). I mean, you can't contact her or interfere with my contacting her in any way, even if you've got me tied up in your apartment for days.
   (I do not mean to be putting ideas in your head, by the way!!!)
   You also – ha ha! – can't mutilate or do anything to permanently disfigure me by tattooing, piercing, etc. (I'm not even sure about "cutting.") Perhaps it is unnecessary to write such things – but I have never been in such a situation before, so I do not know what is necessary to include or preclude. (Of course I am aware that the very mention of such taboo acts may inflame

your desire to perform them – is not this the very essence of perversity? Yet if I don't mention them, would I not be prey to all you might choose to do?)

If you agree to the above paragraph, I will be happy to become what you have requested – till the week before Labor Day, anyway, when the Current is due to return.

> *Anxiously awaiting your reply,*
> *Chris*

38

> *Saturday*

Dear Box 392,

Of course the answer is 'yes'; how could it not be?

I think of you constantly. I imagine you knocking at my door, coming in and raping me. (But of course I could not know that it was you.) (But I would, I am sure.)

Am I scared? Of course, but that cannot equal the fear of not seeing you again. Not just the longing for you, but the moral failure such cowardice would imply. How could I forgive myself? I could not. Who could? This is my war, my Sir Gawain and the Green Knight, my journey into the heart of darkness, after which good deeds my fair lady will reward me for my persistence and courage.

I want to go through that door. I want (I think) to be transformed. But I also want (I think) to come back.

Already I have conquered the first Test – the Terrible Tyranny of the Eye. Suppose you are indeed, as my friend Leslie suggests, unattractive. (She can imagine no other reason for the *blindfold.) I have thought it through. I can live with that (I <u>think</u>) – out of the unusualness and perversity of it.*

Really, it is all about perversity, isn't it? Sex is just the "cos-tume." Really, we are the bravest people in the world.

What I am most petrified of is not death but humiliation. If I were to tell you that I did not trust you, would that make you more trustworthy, or less?

Your would-be sex slave,
Chris

39

Sunday

Dear Box 392,

Although, to the average person, the easy answer would be 'no,' you & I know that the easy answer (for someone like me) is really 'yes,' & I nearly mailed that off yesterday (with some <u>caveats</u>, of course – do you know the meaning? – concerning anonymity & bodily protection) without thinking, but then.... Putting aside the obvious stuff about fear (both physical & men-tal), and a distrust that is willed rather than intuitive (I mean, against all normal presumptions, I have to <u>tell</u> myself to distrust you, instead of doing so <u>naturally</u>), I find, beneath the trust that lies beneath the willed distrust, a <u>further</u> distrust, one that has to do not so much with your character (or even mine) as it has to do with the consequences of what such a pact naturally engenders. I mean, we don't know each other (as my last shrink said: <u>nobody</u> knows each other – we don't even really "know" ourselves), but even if I <u>did</u> know you "utterly & completely" (to *the extent that the aforementioned shrink would agree we can know somebody) that doesn't mean you know how they'll act under future conditions & circumstances – certainly ones they've never encountered before, but possibly even ones they have ("can't walk in the same river twice" etc.). E.g. assuming you've never done such a thing before (& I don't know whether I hope you have or haven't!) you can't know what changes in our hearts and minds and character such a relationship could bring about – & even if you have done such a thing before with someone else, you haven't with me, & the interaction between you & me could create something heretofore unexpected, & possibly dangerous, that at the moment neither you nor I have any possibility of fore-telling!).*

Now in a certain sense I always feel I "know" the future, that nothing is new (which is why my life is so boring), & although I "know" from my (current) shrink that this is false, I think it is something I intuitively feel most of the time (except those rare moments when I am not depressed), & probably that is the reason why I answered your ad in the first place – because it did seem that for once there was something truly new that I didn't know about beforehand. But although one part of me looks forward to this "not knowing," the other part (the "ego," if I may use an outdated term) warns me – "hold on, you don't know the future, you never did, as much as you feel like you 'know' this person you don't (not even what she looks like), & if you don't how can you let her have you completely at her mercy?"

And I don't really know how to answer that question. And until I am able to answer that question, how am I going to be able to commit myself to a contract – or keep the commitment if I make it???

But (on the <u>other</u> hand), I know all this is bullshit, for no other reason than because I could never forgive myself for not following through on this.

Excited but apprehensive,
Chris

40

Dear Box 392,

Because the easy answer is 'yes,' and because I therefore distrust this (as I always distrust the 'easy' way), but because I also distrust the distrust (and maybe even the distrust of the distrust of the distrust) I keep postponing sending you an answer, until I discover what is at the heart of my… confusion.

(But is it possible to discover what is at 'the heart' of all 'this' until I do it – at which point it w/could be 'too late'????)

On the other hand, if to counter my 'natural' inclination is (for me) 'natural' – which would lead the 'average' person to conclude I should 'therefore' say 'no' – perhaps what I should really be countering is my natural inclination for me to counter my 'natural' inclination – & should therefore say 'yes!!!'

Such thinking is delaying my responding to your request. I don't know whether you expected me to respond sooner rather than later (or even if you expected me to respond <u>at all</u>). I don't know what the 'expected' behavior is under such circumstances, & (<u>of course</u>) am therefore torn between appearing pathetically eager and pusillanimously reluctant.

(You <u>do</u> realize, I 'trust,' that my desire to overcome such

self-consciousness is at the heart of my considering such a proposition at all.)

(I do <u>not</u> know why I am writing in such stilted 19th century-like prose: do you?)

I've been having an immense amount of trouble sleeping since I saw you. Images keep crowding through my mind – partly of 'you' (you are blond, you are brunette, you are beautiful, you are ugly, you are brilliant, you're a fool, you're 22, you're 58), partly of myself ('martyr' vs. 'jerk'), partly of my girlfriend (disgusted, titillated), partly of my friends (outraged, envious), even my shrink (trying to conceal her revulsion under the liberal 'tolerant' veneer), etc. I can't figure out whether even the contemplation of such a commitment makes me the bravest person on earth, or whether it means I'm <u>so</u> lazy a person I'll do <u>anything</u> to avoid 'doing the work' (of sex or a relationship), or maybe I'm not lazy so much as so morally cowardly a person that I put the responsibility for all action on someone else – which is why I'm having such trouble making this decision. Usually I make decisions by <u>not</u> making them (but pretending I'll make them in the future), but since in this case the time frame is delineated by the absence of the Current, it is more-than-usually difficult to conceal from myself the fact that in <u>this</u> case 'no decision' means (in fact) a 'no.'

On the other hand....

Please let me know what you think – I mean, your honest and disinterested (if such a thing is possible!) opinion on whether you think I can 'handle' this – & if it's a good idea for me to or not.

Confused,
Chris

41

Dear Box 392,

If your defense is facelessness, mine is anonymity. I know where you live (or at least rent an apartment) but not what you look like; you know so much about the 'inner' me but nothing of the 'outer.' (Or do you?) Which (assuming you don't) evens out the 'power game,' doesn't it?

Let me explain why I haven't answered you sooner.

Fear, of course (not that there is ever a moment when I'm not afraid), not so much of pain but permanent damage or disfigurement, even dying (I am frightened to even say – write – this, lest it put ideas into your head, but of course, what's the point of a relationship like this unless everything can be known?), but even more so (at least, this seems more likely) of falling into a black hole where all I want is you and what we do together (I'm not even sure whether to call this 'sex') and the rest of my life collapses and disappears forever. On one level, of course, this attracts me (for what else does one really enjoy in life except physical sensations?) but it also scares me, not just on the obvious level but on a deeper one – one that may even be deeper than my attraction to it. I mean, if there really is a 'death instinct' (Freud chickened out on this like he did on the seduction theory!) then surely this desire for the black hole is nothing but that. And the 'life instinct' part of me rebels against this, just as, say, on a sunny cold day in winter, in a country house where (despite solemn assurances before your visit) they have sworn to keep the thermostat at 72 but during the night creep down & change it to the mid-60s, you lie in bed for hours in the morning debating *whether to jump out of bed into the freezing room or continue to lie there, & you end up falling sleep for yet another few hours (meaning you'll have a headache all day – too much sleep being as bad as too little!), so too there is this constant war in my soul (perhaps in <u>everybody's</u> soul?) between the instinct to surrender and sleep and the instinct to get up and struggle. Now if pure 'desire' is the key, surely we would dream our lives away (& one can of course take the argument that between illegal drugs, prescription drugs, over-the-counter drugs, alcohol, coffee, tobacco, &, of course, tv – Americans do in fact 'dream' their lives away), & the temptation is to declare that it is only the Puritan aspects that we have ingrained into ourselves (to which we give such names as 'ambition,' 'duty' – even, at times, 'love') that make us rise out of bed to attend the generally insufficiently recompensed, often demeaning, usually irritating, and always time-consuming employment we endure so as to be able to maintain both ourselves and our possessions (& in this I include not just objects and people but domiciles and means of trans- portation both utilitarian – auto – & <u>not</u> – boats, horses, sleds, skis) in the style to which we/they've become accustomed – and not just 'employment' but the endless other duties for the main- tenance & health of the above, including, but not limited to, ever more frequent and expensive visits to doctors, oral hygienists, shrinks, nutritionists, physical therapists, chiropractors, acupunc- turists, health club trainers, masseurs, auto mechanics, computer repairmen, etc. (even in the absence of unusual traumas such as illness, genetic conditions, and accidents which may necessi- tate painful and expensive courses of treatment including body work, the ingestion of toxic drugs, the exposure of one's body to the harmful effects of radiation, etc., often without knowing*

*whether such treatments will assist us in the slightest), plus
<u>further</u> additional expense to purchase insurance policies whose
sole function is to offset some of the costs of the above – and
this we must do not just for ourselves and our possessions but
the disposal of such after death: a conceptual pleasure indeed,
as by definition we will not even be around to benefit by such
arrangements!... and this is how we spend nearly all the waking
moments of our lives....*

*So "to sleep, perchance to dream" – to partake of the lotus
flower and fall into that black hole (the womb?) from whence
one may not return – so seductive is this thought, so impossible
the idea that one could ever (once exposed) abandon such
delights, that I wonder whether I any longer have the strength
to overcome what must be the immense power of that learned
resistance that has kept me so long from succumbing to my
dreams. Indeed, to deal with this is to come face-to-face with
that most important (and despairing!) of all questions – The
Meaning of Life....*

*To wit: I fear that at the end of the summer when I go back
to my 'ordinary life' there won't be one there, that the Current
will leave me, that, unable to tolerate 'vanilla' sex, I'll never again
find anyone to satisfy me and that I will dream about what happened with you for the rest of my life. I'm afraid of going insane,
having a breakdown, spending the rest of my life in a mental
hospital – & I'm afraid that, in some weird horrible bizarre way,
I might <u>want</u> this, as a way out of the tedium and repetition I
seem increasingly unable to cope with. I'm frightened, most of
all, by the terrible emptiness inside me that craves you, that
craves intensity, that craves whatever is forbidden and disgusting, that feels like it wants to be overwhelmed so completely*

there's nothing the part I call 'me' can do anything about.

(There are also fears of a more "superficial" nature – that you are doing all this to blackmail me, that you will take pictures of me and sell them to magazines, that the contrast with my ordinary life will make me unable to function. (To be honest, this is <u>already</u> happening, though, to be even <u>more</u> honest, hardly for the first time), etc.)

But there is also a contrary (or perhaps, <u>contradictory</u>) fear, and that is, rather than forever being in thrall to the powers of the goddess Aphrodite, what if I am <u>not</u>? What if, after a period of time with you, it turns out I am <u>not</u> the most ravenous of sexual beings but just an ordinary kind of person with the standard amount and type of desires & fears, that what drew me to you was not some kind of uniqueness but on the contrary some vain attempt to escape this ordinariness? (One could of course argue that a desire to escape ordinariness is itself evidence that one is not 'ordinary,' but much as I wish to subscribe to such a belief, honesty compels me to admit that it is more likely merely evidence of a paralyzing self-consciousness that can be said to partake of the extraordinary only in the extent of its manifestations. . . .) Is it not perhaps better to live with the dream of my possible extraordinariness than to risk the possibility of having to recognize my own banality? (Indeed, is it not practically <u>proof</u> of my banality that I would even have such a fear?) Does not every sentence that I write provide further proof that I am unworthy of such a pact?

Totally confused,
Chris

42

Dear Box 392,

*I've been analyzing what's taken me so long to write –
especially as the 'reply,' in any real sense, was 'ordained.' Was
it the so-called Rational Mind putting up the good fight or rather,
my 'lip service' to the Rational Mind – so that I could provide
'evidence' that I put up 'the good fight'? Actually, now I think of
it, it's not rational to continue fighting if you know you're going to
'lose' anyway – it's yet another form of Masochism (that in this
case detracts from the real masochism, i.e. my time with you).
Maybe it was just a way of punishing myself for my unconscious
desire to be with you. Or, rather, perhaps it was a way to prolong
the anticipation, the 'suspense' (I am speaking of the rather
technical literary definition of the word – where the mystery is not
the identity of the culprit but rather how to apprehend him/her),
to titillate me so much that when I finally make some kind of
'contract' with you & I get really petrified (as I'm sure I will) I'll
have this extra residue of desire to carry me along. Maybe it's
because I can't feel desire without frustration. Maybe it's some
weird kind of 'homage' to all those years when I wanted to sleep
with women and couldn't tell anyone and the desire to do so
built up and up and up so that for years the pleasure of the
release of <u>talking</u> about it became almost sexual. Maybe it was
to prolong my (albeit relative) 'innocence' – those last moments
before the commencing of our strange relationship which I
suspect/know/hope? will change everything utterly. (I already
have a feeling of 'nostalgia' for <u>those</u> days, which of course, till
I see you, are '<u>these</u>' days.)*

Of course I've been wondering what (& _if_) you were thinking about me – whether you thought I would or wouldn't contact you, whether you knew it would take time or not, whether you even cared – maybe even _suffered_ – at my absence, the way I was suffering at yours. (So maybe, after all, this delay was a way of punishing _you_!) Sometimes while masturbating I'd imagining you were masturbating too, thinking of me: I'd squeeze my eyes real hard to project my thoughts into you. Did you feel this? I wonder if you'll ever tell me (but of course you won't) – or, rather, even if you told me how would I know it was 'the truth'? (Sometimes I wonder whether I even _want_ to know!) Maybe it's more exciting – or at least more _interesting_ (& is there a dif-ference?) not to. Because, after all, the worst forms of torture (unless – god forbid! – our experience together proves me wrong!) are mental. For, at 'bottom' this strange dance we're commencing is not about the body _at all_, but an 'intellectual' investigation into desire/sensation whose method of analysis takes the outward form of 'sex.' To put it another way, it's an 'intellectual' curiosity about a – _seemingly_ – non-intellectual desire – an intellectual curiosity that can only be explored by the performance of certain physical acts (which then become the 'investigative techniques'). But the ultimate point isn't even epistemological, but _metaphysical_ – can one bond with another so as to escape the terrifying loneliness of The Void? Or is there, in fact, nothing really there but projection and illusion (but at least that might make Death more acceptable!)?

Do you agree?

In this sense, the more complicated the dance, the 'better' – because it sustains curiosity. (Is Life then _only_ about not being bored?) Of course there's the more sentimental interpretation –

an End to Loneliness and so on, about discovering whether I am really the 'sickest' person in the universe, or whether someone else will say, 'Yeah, that thought has occurred to me too – <u>and stuff even worse</u>!'

(I sometimes wonder if there's anything <u>in the world</u> I haven't thought of!)

I'm afraid also that this is putting too much on you, that no matter how spectacular the acts that occur between us are they will not only <u>not</u> be able to rescue me from that terrible sense of emptiness and meaninglessness that has been with me my entire life (at least as far as I remember) – but they would <u>never</u> be able to do so because of my own apparent mental (metaphysical?) limitations! That is, even if in some sense the Universe does have 'meaning,' I would not be able to perceive it, so after all the horrendous things have been done, I will end up with… nothing. <u>Absolutely nothing</u>! No transcendence, no transformation, nothing but a horrible emptiness… <u>forever</u>!!!.

But <u>worse</u> than before – as even this extreme method will have failed!

I fear, also, September, when the Current comes back, the contract ends, and I return to my 'real' life and all that this entails: guilt, longing, (not for 'you' exactly, but what you represent, but which I might very well 'interpret,' in my usual Romantic way, to <u>be</u> You) – insomnia, crying, more boredom with sex than usual… and then, sometime in the future, after Couples Therapy or a night of drinking, the inevitable Confession and all the recriminations, apologies, etc. this entails… followed by the Grand Forgiveness, followed by….

Is this misery worth it? For you must understand, as certain *as I am & have always been that I will ultimately go through with this, I'm just as certain I will never let what happens between you and me interfere with my 'real life.' Indeed, the predetermined ending date, the knowledge of a specific time at which satisfaction must end, the elimination of that hideous ambivalence that accompanies the slow withdrawal of passion & all the questions and anxiety as to whether one should see the person yet one more time, is utterly crucial to the structure of this peculiar 'relationship.' Does not a definitive ending guarantee the prolongation of desire? What can I not agree to, if I know it is merely 'temporary'? How can there be boredom, if this is merely a respite from the routine boredom of my life rather than the beginning of yet another routine...? Finally, does not the knowledge of the End to Satisfaction ensure a permanent nostalgia for it – even as it is in the process of happening – and is not nostalgia the most powerful of emotions?*

To put it another way: if undergoing an experiment like ours is the only way I am able to find meaning and pleasure, how will I be able to live the rest of my life once that is over???

Forgive my delayed response and the length of this letter. But I feel, before we commence, I must express myself to you utterly, so that you know all of me – not just my body but my thoughts and feelings and emotions and methods of disguising (and revealing!) all of the above. If I look like a jerk, so be it! I am tired of this endless pretense toward 'cool' or 'hip' or whatever the word is now. See? I don't even know it! (Of course, you could say my admission of 'lack of cool' is just another, even more complicated way of evincing 'cool' – by such a demonstration of indifference to it. But perhaps that is pushing it.)

Hot, wet, consumed and terrified by desire (but more so by its fear of loss)

Your partner in darkness,
Chris

43

Thursday

Dear Box 392,
Surely you knew this waiting was part of the game. Surely you will punish me as you see fit. Surely you know everything and thus know there is no need to punish me.

I await your commands.
Chris

44

Tuesday

Dear Chris,
Friday at 8. Wear your Calvins.

45

Upon opening the letter I saw, of course, how vain my labors had been. Surely, no matter which one letter I had sent, she would have answered with precisely the same short (only *apparently* unironic) note.

Seven-thirty that evening, having drunk two beers, in front of a particularly outrageous sunset, I went down to the pier, a third can of beer in a brown bag, and sat there until the sky was a deep purple and lights were on in front and behind and above me. A Walkperson was around my ears but I did not turn it on. I listened to the jokes and boomboxes and I asked god to give me a sign as to whether or not I should really go to her apartment on Friday.

But the question was as bullshitty as my torment over "The Writing of the Letters." From the time I started writing her, or even when she had made her request (perhaps even from the moment I first answered the ad), there had never really been a question I would see it through to wherever it took me. Partly because I wouldn't forgive myself if I didn't, partly because I had spent so much time writing the letters, and partly because it was summer, and summer doesn't count.

3.
The Contract

46

I had thought so much about her that being with her no longer felt strange, but the place I went to every night in bed when I shut my eyes.

And not just at night. In the day, every time I blinked and took a tiny little vacation from the world.

"It's good to be here," I said. "I've missed you."

"Of course."

"It's not that I didn't keep thinking of you. I kept rewriting the letters. But I was scared."

"You should be. A contract is different, there's no backing out. You may ask to renegotiate, of course, but I don't have to acquiesce. Even so, there would be penalties."

"What kind of penalties?"

"If that's the focus of your concern, you shouldn't be here."

"It's not. But my mind says it should be. I mean, if I were telling this to somebody else, they would say it ought to be. They would think I'm crazy to even consider this."

"Perhaps that's why you've waited so long to realize your true nature."

My 'true' nature? Was this my true nature? Or a vacation from it?

"I've never known anyone who did anything like this."

"Surely at least some of your friends have."

"Are you crazy?"

"Don't talk to me like that." She flicked my throat with the whip.

"Sorry."

"They probably just don't talk about it with you."

"We talk about everything."

"Really?"

Now that I thought about it, only Leslie knew about my visits here – and she didn't know much. "You like to think you're so unusual, Chris. But you're not."

Could it be possible there was a world out there that every-body knew about but me? Could it be possible that some of my friends had kneeled in this very same way, to her or someone she knew? What if one of them, say Leslie, had 'recommended' me? Could that be why she had chosen me, rather than some-body else?

It was a horrifying idea, not just because it would mean everyone I knew had been deceiving me, but if I had not known about this, surely there were other things I didn't know about as well....

But it was also reassuring – because it would mean that what I was doing was not 'crazy,' but something anyone would do.

"There were a lot of responses to the ad," she continued.

"I wondered."

"Slaves come a dime a dozen. I had to make my decision carefully." As we were talking, she was casually attaching breast clamps to my nipples. As I knew, these had to be very tight or else they would fall off.

"Was I the only one you met? Or were there others?"

"You don't expect me to answer that, do you?"

I gasped with pain. "No." The clamps were linked together with a little chain, and pulling on this really hurt.

"Why me?"

"Instinct." I lay my head back on the couch, my throat totally exposed. She stroked my Adam's apple softly, almost tickling, so that I was unable to remain still. Although I begged her to touch me, she wouldn't, but merely continued this odd stroking, occasionally pressing her hand against my throat in a way that made me cough, as if gasping for breath, although somehow it was also oddly soothing.

She pushed me off her. Her voice came from above. "I'll be back in a few minutes. Please wait for me on your knees."

It is not that easy to get in a kneeling position with your hands fastened behind your back, but I did. I listened to her footsteps, and then in the distance, a drawer being opened. Music from cars on the street grew louder and faded away. I could hear music in the building also, some laughter from (perhaps) a neighboring fire escape. Some people were cooking something on a little barbecue. A toilet was flushing. Water from a sink. Her footsteps returning.

A few seconds later, there was a searing sensation, as the clamps popped off my breasts. I gasped. As the pain wore off, I became conscious of a duller pain in my knees, which grew worse the more I concentrated on it. But she noticed when I tried to relax backwards for a second, and yanked my arms back in a pain that was neither satisfying nor soothing.

"Chris, you are here to make a contract?" she asked.

"Yes."

"I will tell you what is required, and tell me if you will be able to acquiesce or not. In turn, you will tell me what you require. Think carefully. Once we agree, there is no backing out."

Her tone was grave. I could tell, from the language, either she had planned very carefully what she was going to say, or else she had said it (perhaps many times!) before. "You will be my slave twenty-four hours a day, seven days a week, till the termination of the contract, which shall be Labor Day at midnight."

"A week before the Current returns—"

"Yes. This will give you to time to repair whatever wounds – physical or psychic – you may have. And do not mistake, you will have them."

"The pain doesn't bother me. But I don't want my body permanently altered in any way. No piercing or tattooing. No putting dyes in cuts. And what we do mustn't interfere with my personal or professional life in any way."

"The pain will bother you. I'd be failing in my duty to you if it did not. And what we do may permanently alter you, and interfere with your life in ways you cannot imagine, even if it's not always visible to the naked eye."

"That's okay. I just meant—"

"Don't say 'okay' so casually. I want you to really think about it one last time, before you can no longer change your mind. I want the full consciousness of what you're doing – the shame and the degradation that you're submitting yourself to, the pain of what you will undergo, the humiliations that you will experience, the patheticness of your being that could want to do something like this to be fully apparent to you now, so that you can never pretend – not to me, of course, because I'm not buying – but to yourself and to whomever you may now or someday choose to confide in, that you did not in full consciousness and possession of your mental faculties, with unimpaired ability to calculate consequence and risk, arrive at your decision?"

"I did."

"Without undue external pressure or influence of any sort?"

"No—"

"Including drugs of any sort, whether administered by me or not—"

"No—"

"Or alcohol—"

"Of course not."

"Nor temporary physical passion inspired by my proximity?"

"No."

"In light of all this, what is your reasoned and dispassionate decision?"

"Like I said, I agree to the contract."

"In other words, you will temporarily be my slave, doing whatever I ask you to do, not doing those things I tell you not to do, participating in whatever sexual or other acts as I see fit, obeying me happily in all particulars, whether in my presence or not, until the time—"

"What do you mean, 'in your presence or not'?"

"I mean that a slave is a slave, whether her owner is physically present or not. It is a state of mind, a mode of being, in which the physical is merely an objective correlative of the internal reality. On my part, in return for your surrender and trust, I promise not to seriously injure or kill you or cause permanent bodily disfiguration or harm, to cease all acts immediately should you lose consciousness, to get you immediate medical attention should such ever be necessary, and if at some point I feel that you are physically or psychically unable to continue this contract, I will terminate it. But you must understand, I'll be the one to decide if that point is reached, not you."

She paused. The breeze from the open window chilled my sweat. I breathed deeply, with my mouth open, for I was not getting enough oxygen.

"I'm nervous," I said. I coughed, not because I really needed to clear my throat, but because the sound reassured me I existed.

"Of course." She wiped the hair from my eyes, the gesture that more than anything comforts me. I could feel her fingers around my eyes, feeling the wet. "It's an incredibly big step you're making. Surely the biggest of your life."

Although I told myself it was corny, I felt scared. "Have you really done this before?" I asked.

"Have *you* done this before?" she replied.

We were silent. "There are no testimonials here. You are entering a world in which it is just you and me. I could have participated in a hundred relationships just like this, and all of them might have ended in...death. I could have had a hundred relationships like this, all of which were incredibly exciting and... 'life-affirming.' But no matter what has or has not happened in the past, how could that guarantee that nothing disastrous might not happen between you and me? There are no guarantees in life, Chris. I know you're smarter than that."

As she spoke, I realized I had never done anything that took real courage. The things I had done that looked like they had been brave had been done offhandedly, without thinking, often with a willed refusal to think. Because I was a writer and spent much time thinking, I had assumed that in some sense I was a philosopher – a person who is conscious of the implications of her words and actions – but in the moments of my life that had counted I had been a zombie.

My brain was saying: 'This is something you have always wanted. This is something you have always been afraid of. If you do not do this now, you will never do it.' The thought of doing something courageous, in total consciousness of my fear of it, sent a surge of adrenaline through me.

"I have a collar for you to wear. It's the symbol of our agree-ment, and is emblematic of your absolute submission to me, the fact that you agree to do whatever I want you to do, without refusal or complaint, within the limits of our contract. You'll wear it for the length of our contract – not just when you're here, but all the time, night and day, in your house or outside. When the contract is over you'll have to give it back. It has a little lock only I have the key to. Whenever you look in the mirror, you'll remem-ber who it is that owns you. Once I put this on it will be too late to back out."

She lay the collar upon my skin. It was metal, cool and heavy, definitive and cold. I yearned to be wearing it, to have a symbol proclaiming who and what I was to all the world.

"Please put it on me," I said.

I bowed my head, as if I were going to be sacrificed. The metal was more supple than I would have thought, for it draped itself around the curves of my neck as she drew it tight, slightly squeezing my Adam's Apple. I started to cough but couldn't. I told myself to be calm and breathe through my nose. Meanwhile she pulled it even tighter. 'She's going to kill me,' I thought. 'I deserve it.' I did not see stars, but the screen-saver pattern of my Windows program. I did not try to resist; perhaps I did not care.

She loosened the collar. Then I heard a little click. "Very good," I heard as if distantly.

I gulped air. Once I realized I was not going to die, that the collar in fact did not hurt but was only a bit uncomfortable, that it conformed pleasantly to the curves of my neck, a kind of warm rush went through my insides – part relief, part gratitude, part excitement – but also, oddly, disappointment.

"I am proud of you Chris," she said. "This is going to prove an enjoyable interlude, for both of us." The word 'interlude' made me sad.

"I thought, for a moment, you were going to kill me."

"It would be counter-productive, wouldn't it, to deprive myself of the use of my property?"

This was an unsatisfying answer. I kneeled there for a while, awkward with the silence and the position, increasingly conscious of my knees.

"What are you doing?" she suddenly asked.

"Nothing."

"You've changed position, haven't you?"

Only now did I realize I had sat back on my heels, easing the stress on my knees, lower back, and quads. "I'm sorry," I said. "It was unconscious."

"That doesn't make it better." I got back in position, but the respite – allowing blood to flow more freely – only made the pain worse. "When I tell you to get in a position, you stay in it, until I tell you to move or you'll ask me permission to move and I give it to you."

"Yes."

"Yes, *sir*. This is how you are to address me in the future." "Yes, *sir*."

Something stung my ass. "Do I detect a note of sarcasm in your voice?"

"No, *sir*."

"Get that smirk out of your voice."

"Yes sir."

"That's better. Try again."

"Yes, sir."

"Good."

I burst out in embarrassed giggles.

"You find this amusing?" she asked.

"No. . . ." But I could not stop myself. "It's just – it's so *corny*. The language. The collar. Like an old-fashioned porno movie."

Something stung my ass again. "Is this corny too?"

"In a way." She struck me again.

"Has it occurred to you, Chris, that maybe *you* are the one who's corny? That maybe it's *you* whose desires are banal, corny, and predictable? That you're no different from all the other slaves in the city?"

"No."

"Think about it. Think about how you can distinguish yourself for me, so that this will be as interesting for me as it is for you. What I'm doing is very hard work, extraordinarily hard work, requiring time and effort and imagination and research, which is why there are so many more people willing to be in your position than in mine."

"What do you mean – 'research'?"

"Which kind of collar can be worn for weeks without chafing. Which kind of wrist restraints will not cut the skin or unduly inhibit circulation. Which kind of paddles and whips create the greatest sensations while minimizing the visible results of their employment."

"I would hardly call that 'research,'" I said.

"You certainly are in a frisky mood," she said. We sat in silence awhile. "What kind of 'reward' do you think such comments should bring?"

"I don't know. That's your job."

"My job," she said, running her fingers oh so lightly up the sides of my breasts, "is to play you like a violin." She moved her fingers up and down, up and down, and this soft random stroking was more arousing in this context than something more genital would have been. "Often you will be choosing your own punishment, and it will be interesting to see how far you are willing to take yourself – not just in the pain of that choice, but the shame of having chosen it. So, what punishment will you choose now, for yourself?"

"I don't know." What came to my mind was either so banal or so perverse I could not say it.

"You surprise me. I know how much you pride yourself on your intelligence and imagination – not just here but in your so-called 'line of work.'"

Was she trying to tell me she knew who I was? "What do you mean?" I asked.

"You know what I mean," she said. "Don't play the naïf with me, or you'll have me regretting my choice. You were chosen for a *reason*, you know."

"I thought it was because of my cute ass."

She waited a moment, then an incredibly sharp sting, like a snake of liquid fire, curled around my ass. As it struck, I recalled the slight whistling through air I had just heard.

"Ahhhh!" I screamed.

"Your ass isn't so cute anymore."

"Oh." I was gasping and sweating. Whereas her normal spankings – no matter how much they hurt – had somehow managed to remain in the realm of the 'idea' of punishment, this stroke was pure pain.

"It's time to take this seriously," she said. "You're here to learn lessons you can learn in no other way. This is one place words won't help you out of."

I heard the ticking of a clock, the refrigerator clicking on and off. I waited for her to speak, but she did not. Gradually the silence became a battlefield between us. I resolved I would not open my mouth before she would, that I would win the first battle of our wills as (in some sense) I would win all the others. The one thing I knew how to do in the world was endure. I held my breath, to listen to her breathing. The floor gave slightly, with a slight creak or sigh, as she pushed herself against it and stood up. I heard her walk away.

Music came on. My knees were killing me. It seemed safe, so I sat back on my heels. The liquid serpent struck again – this time against my back.

"Ow! Don't do that!" I shouted. I screamed, but as the initial shock receded, I felt a kind of reassurance, at how much attention she paid to what I did.

"If you don't calm yourself, Chris, I'll have to gag you. Now get on your knees like I told you."

In various kinds of pain, both large and small, dull and sharp, my knees aching, I struggled into position. I wondered if the liquid on my back was blood or sweat.

"Don't ever think I won't know when you disobey me," she said. "Because I will. And when I don't, you'll tell me. You'll *want* to tell me. You'll *need* to tell me." She stood behind me and cradled my head against her stomach. Her fingers pressed my throat below the necklace, as if to remind me of that moment earlier when it was almost choking me.

"Would you like a cookie?" she asked, almost sweetly.

"Yes," I said, not so much because I was hungry, but out of

gratitude. I heard a bag opening, then a soft crunching. "Open your mouth," she commanded. I could feel the hard edge of a cookie touching my lip.

But nothing happened. I felt like a dog, begging for a treat from its master. Instead, I could hear her chewing. I was about to shut my mouth to swallow when something did pass between my lips. But it was no cookie, or rather, it *was* a cookie, but not a nice fresh cookie, but the soggy chewed-up mess that had been in her mouth. I started to gag.

"Swallow it," she ordered. "You said you wanted a cookie."

My stomach rebelling, my throat refusing to give me saliva to aid in the task, my body sweating, it took me awhile to be able to swallow it. I told myself this was nothing different than kissing someone and then eating a cookie, yet my body refused to believe it.

"You'd probably like to rinse your mouth out with water," she asked.

"Yes…. Yes sir," I said.

She spit into my mouth, and I had to swallow this too.

"Now that we've covered the basics, I guess it's time to get down to business. I'd like you to stand up… No, wait. I guess there is one more thing," she said, perhaps too casually.

"Yes?"

"It's probably irrelevant, for I'm sure the idea of breaking the contract has never occurred to you—"

"No," I lied. But even as she had fastened the collar around my neck, I was thinking: *I can break the contract if I really need to; it's not like it's enforceable in a court of law.*

"So I can trust you to keep it?"

"I gave my word."

"Then you won't mind there being . . . a little penalty if at some point in the future you decide you've made a mistake and try to ignore our agreement?"

My heart began beating faster. "What kind of penalty?"

"It hardly matters, does it, since you've absolutely assured me you wouldn't break your word. Just a formality."

"Like what?"

"You tell me. What do you think would be fair?"

"I guess I could write you a check," I said. "A teller's check to 'cash.' Which means I'd be trusting *you*. And you could promise to cash it only if I break my word."

"That's an interesting idea, Chris," she said thoughtfully. "What size check do you have in mind?"

"I don't know."

"But that's the heart of the matter, isn't it? You weren't thinking of something like a hundred dollars, I presume?"

"Five hundred dollars. A thousand?" I hazarded.

"A thousand dollars, for breaking your word. My, my! You don't seem to put a very high value on your word."

"Okay. Two thousand," I said.

"How about five thousand, Chris, or ten?"

"That's too much!"

"Your word isn't worth ten thousand dollars?"

"It's not like I have ten thousand dollars in the bank. Or five. If you don't believe me, I'll go with you to a cash machine. . . . Anyway, what's to prevent you from cashing it anyway? I don't even know your name."

"Do I know yours, 'Chris'??? You'll trust me with your life, but not a check for ten thousand dollars?"

She moved behind me. I felt her cool hands on my neck and

I thrust my weight against her. I let out a deep breath. "I trust you," I said. "I just don't know how I'd be able to explain it to the Current—"

She laughed. "This is not about money, Chris," she said, supporting my body with one hand and gently caressing my throat. "For once you're in something money won't be able to get you out of. I had a slightly different idea...."

"What?"

"If you break the contract, I no longer respect the privacy of our agreement."

It was a different 'oh.' "But you promised!" I tried to straighten up, but she held me, still stroking.

"And you promised to keep your contract." She leaned over, and pressing my head against her a bit awkwardly, kissed me gently on the lips. I opened my mouth and welcomed her upside-down tongue – a few crumbs still sticking to it – into my mouth. For the first time, perhaps, in my life, I felt I was with someone as foresightful and witty as me.

Still supporting me, she stood up. I lay with my head against her legs, a feeling of utter peace coursing through my being. She lightly circled my Adam's apple with her finger, then very gradually increased the pressure of the tickling. Then the tickling stopped, and there was just pressure. I didn't resist her – it didn't occur to me to resist – I just breathed slowly and deeply into the pressure and the slight pain, succumbing to the pleasant feeling of lightheadedness and the pretty screen saver patterns. I wasn't scared, but felt a great comfort at the thought of my life being in her hands. If I was to die, so be it.

"You *are* special, Chris," she said. "I have a feeling this can be special."

"I love you," I said.

"No you don't."

47

"And when you thought about being here, what was it you imagined?" As before, she'd led me down the hall, to what I assumed was the bedroom, for I was lying on my back on a mattress. My hands were each attached separately to the bed, as was the right leg. The left leg was free.

"The usual stuff," I said. "Nothing interesting."

"What usual stuff?"

"What I probably thought most about was you telling me your name, and how old you were, and what you did for a living if, in fact, you do anything for a living. And what you look like, of course."

"And if you could know just one of these, Chris, which would it be?"

"What you look like, I guess," I admitted reluctantly.

"What if it turns out you don't like the way I look and you're stuck in this contract with me? Wouldn't it be better for you to remain 'in the dark' about something as crucial as that?"

"Maybe," I admitted. "I couldn't enjoy this if I knew you were unattractive."

"How can what I look like have anything to do with whether or not you're *enjoying* this – as you so oddly put it? Perhaps I should show you what I look like, if only to increase your sufferings."

So she really *was* unattractive. Although this was the most obvious reason for someone to conceal herself, I was somehow still surprised. I had only been allowed to touch her a little, yet nothing in what I had felt was inconsistent with my image of her as young Elvis. The hair a little longer, maybe, but it could have grown. It would bother me a lot, I realized, to give up that fantasy.

I felt exhausted, as if I had put forth a huge effort that had not been recognized, and was also angry – both at her and myself – and I wondered what I'd do to get through the subsequent weeks. Would it really matter if she didn't respect my privacy? She probably didn't know who I was, or, even if she did, or found out in the future, what would it matter?

I could say I did it for the experience, to help in my writing. It was even true, perhaps.

I could join the Current in Sweden, and deal with this later.

"Aren't there reasons people conceal who they are other than because they're not attractive? I notice you don't carry any forms of identification with you when you come here, yet I have the feeling you don't consider yourself unattractive."

"You look in my pockets?" This remark revived me on several counts: first, by hinting at a reason for concealment other than ugliness, second, because it was a further demonstration of the pleasing deviousness of her mind, and third, because why would she look in my pockets if she knew who I was?

"Don't sound so surprised. If you didn't anticipate my doing so, why would you have left your wallet at home?"

"Just in case."

"We could make a deal. I'll let you know what you'd most like to know about me, if you'll let me know what I'd most like to know about you."

"Which is what?"

"Do we have a deal or not?"

"*No*." She ordered me to resume telling my fantasies. "Actually, part of my fantasy is that you know what I want *without* my telling you my fantasies."

"Unfortunately for you, that is not *my* fantasy."

"Well, I guess part of it was being tied up like this…."

"Yes…."

"And part of it was your talking to me and telling me to do things…."

"Yes…."

"And part of it was your telling me to tell you what you should tell me to do…."

"Yes…."

"And I refuse. But you make me…."

"Yes…."

"And part of it was your spanking – well, paddling me – with a very hard paddle, and then afterwards softly putting some cool gel on my ass and rubbing me gently and telling me what a good girl I am."

"Yes…."

"And part of it was your fucking me with a dildo…not just in the regular place but…."

"Yes…."

"And of course, you call me all kinds of names."

"What kind of names?"

"Slut, whore, bitch, cunt…the standard—"

"This is pretty tame, Chris. Hardly worthy of you. That is, if you are who I think you are."

"Well, not so much names as…oh, you'll tell me how bad I want it, that I'll do anything to get laid, that there's never been such a little slut as me, that I drip like a faucet when you're near me, that I have such a monstrously big hole it's unlikely there's a cock big enough in the universe to touch both sides at once, that I'm such a horny bitch I'd fuck anybody in the world...." I couldn't tell what was more embarrassing – the banality of my thoughts or my mode of expressing them.

"Including Charlie?" She whistled. I could hear the clanking. "You haven't forgotten Charlie, have you?" she asked.

"No."

"I noticed you forgot to include him in your little parade of images."

"I didn't think about him." This was a lie, of course. I had gotten wet many times thinking of Charlie.

"I don't believe you. Lying is as bad as saying 'no,'" she said. "Are you lying, Chris?"

"No." She bit my cheek. Hot waves went through me. "Yes," I whispered.

"Oh, Chris." It was almost a moan. "And what is it about Charlie that makes you so...so...like a river?" she said, her hand on my thigh.

"I don't know," I said.

She slapped my face. "Answer me."

"I think I want him to...I mean, I don't want him to but I keep thinking—"

"What?"

"His long tongue inside me," I whispered. "I think it would... bring me someplace I've never been."

"Where?"

"I don't know."

She slapped the bed. Charlie jumped up on it. "It's lucky,

then, that Charlie likes girls, almost as much as I do, don't you, Charlie?" Charlie barked. I could feel his fur tickling my groin.

Inanely, I began giggling.

"So Charlie's funny, huh? Charlie, she thinks you're funny."

"It tickles."

"Nicely, or not so nice?"

"Kind of nice."

"Stop thrashing, and turn your head to one side." I tried to lie still as a huge tongue grazed my lips and drooled warm saliva in my ear. As a sensation it was pleasant enough, if one could forget what it represented. Then I thought of germs, and I shook my head, the way a dog does when it awakes from a nap, or comes out of the water.

"I said, hold still."

"Dogs have diseases."

"In that case I'd start worrying about places other than my ear."

"No," I moaned, kicking my free leg to keep Charlie away.

She pinned my leg down with part of her body. "I mean it," she said. "You're not to move unless I tell you." She bit my cheek, hard, then got off my leg. It trembled as I tried to hold it still. The hot saliva began falling on other parts of my body, and I felt the softness of Charlie's fur.

"Spread your leg, Chris."

"I can't…." It was a moan of embarrassment rather than denial.

"Of course you can. Charlie is a big dog, you know. Part Dane, part Shepherd, part Husky."

My body was writhing, in excitement and shame. I was panting. I could feel my sweat mingling with the saliva. Any minute

I was going to urinate.

"This can't be happening."

"It is."

"Not just that it's happening, but—"

"What?"

"It's almost like...I want him to."

"But of course you do, Chris. Was there ever a doubt?"

"It's sick."

"In that case we'd better not do it. Charlie," she snapped her fingers, and Charlie jumped off the bed.

I lay there, my body, bucking. "I'm so frustrated," I whined.

"It doesn't seem like anything can satisfy you, Chris. You want Charlie, you don't want him...."

"You could put your hand inside me."

"I could." She lay her hand lightly on me, but didn't put it inside. "I'm not sure it would be fair, however."

"Why?"

"Because it was Charlie that aroused you, not me. It doesn't seem fair to him, and of course, I don't like to be used as some surrogate."

I moaned.

"Do you want my hand inside you, Chris? Is that what you really want?"

"I want...I want...."

"What?"

"Charlie," I whispered.

"Do you?"

"*Yes.*"

"What about the germs—"

I moaned. "Don't do this to me."

"But it's not up to me. You believe in animal rights, don't you Chris?"

"Of course."

"Then don't you think Charlie should have some say in the matter?"

"I suppose." I was whimpering.

"He's a sensitive dog. Maybe you should show him you like him."

"How?"

"How do you usually show someone you like them?"

"I . . . touch them."

"Charlie, come back on the bed." This time, when Charlie jumped up, I moved my left leg toward him.

"I thought I told you to lie still, unless I gave you permission."

"May I move my leg?" I asked.

"*Please*."

"*Please*, may I move my leg?"

"Please *sir*."

"Please *sir*, may I move my leg?"

"*You may.*"

I began to move my foot slowly over Charlie's body. I could feel the fur against my feet, the warmth of his skin, the firmness of his body pressing back. I pushed my foot against his belly, then I moved it up to his mouth.

Charlie began licking my foot. Women had occasionally done this to me, but Charlie's tongue was far larger and softer. I was torn between the urge to laugh hysterically, and control myself so I wouldn't have an orgasm.

"Oh god. Please stop. Please stop." It was definitely not a red code plea, but it tickled so much I tried to pull my foot away.

"Don't."

I fought to hold my leg still. I heard myself whimpering – "uh uh" – very softly. My stomach was clenched, as if I were doing sit-ups.

Charlie stopped.

"I think Charlie likes you," she said. "There's a good indication of that."

"Oh." It was a moan.

"You can't see it. But you could feel it. Surely you want to reciprocate. Don't be selfish."

I moved my foot along his body until I could feel his protrusion. It wasn't hairy, like I expected, but smooth and warm. In itself it was not much, but the idea of it was and intense flashes of energy seemed to make its way from him to me. Meanwhile Charlie began barking. Behind my eyes was orange and red, a fantastic sunset. My leg was trembling. Her hand was now inside my body, and I could not have lain still had she threatened to cut off my head.

"Wider." My right leg was bound, but I moved my left leg out to the side so that it was almost at a right angle to my body.

Behind the sunset, I was vaguely aware of the clanking of the collar, the words "...here, Charlie, here..." then the hot breath of the animal.

"Oh...oh...." I felt the flick of a tongue. It was a flame inside, an immensely soft but searing wet flame. "Oh...oh...."

This incredible warmth was on my vagina, warm and wet but I did not mind the germs. "Ah...ah...ah...." I could hear noises in the distance, both sighs and moans. It was not me making the noise, but it got louder and louder. "Ah...oh...my god, my god...."

"Talk to him," she said.

"Charlie," I whispered. "Charlie...." She took my left leg and placed it on his back. I pressed down, holding Charlie to me. He snuffled. "No, oh no." But I continued pressing him to me. "Stop. Please stop...." The voice that came from me was sobbing.

"No."

"Please...please...I can't...I can't...please...I've got to red code...."

"Not now."

"Yes, now. Red code. Red code."

"You're sure?"

And Charlie was pulled away.

"No...I...not now...but...help me...." It was a frail strange voice I heard, from a place usually far away, the part that never lets go, the part that's afraid to die, that's frightened of every sensation and emotion, that's afraid of urinating, shitting, vomiting, having the insides of my body fall out if I come, *really* come – not by what is ordinarily meant by that word, that little thing people do with their fingers or vibrators or shower faucets or even partners but that other thing, that momentously big thing we always shy away from....

"It's okay."

"I don't want to die."

"You won't."

"I *will*."

"I'm here. Let go...it's okay...."

And so it happened. A huge hot wave engulfed my body, moved through my veins and muscles and tendons up through my neck, then out the top of my head where its energy got lost in the universe. I screamed. Fluid spurted out of me. I blacked out.

48

I staggered out the door, the collar around my neck. In the nearest store window I tried to look at it reflected in the glass. But it was not really bright enough, and the reflection of the streetlights and the buildings across the street and cars made it all but impossible to see.

But I could feel it, a shiny band of metal around my neck, cooling my skin in the hot summer night.

49

Up in my apartment, after forcing myself to pull Esmeralda – lying on her back, her paws outstretched – along the floor in our 'greeting' ritual, I went into the bathroom and turned on the light.

The collar was thin, shiny and beautiful, with a delicate little lock. I could not tell what kind of metal it was – platinum, perhaps, or a very dull silver, or maybe even a kind of white gold. I felt sad at the thought that I would someday have to give it back.

I pulled off my shirt. Despite the incredible pain, the serpent's tail left hardly a trace on my body. If anything, I was less visibly marked than usual.

First I showered, then I poured a lukewarm bath which I filled with the French bath oil. I was beyond exhaustion, in a state more devoid of anxiety than any I had experienced without the aid of some ingested substance. My thoughts had no content, save that of astonishment and gratitude. Only the memory of Charlie was disturbing, but I blanked his image with a fuzzy black square when it popped into my mind.

The collar was too tight for me to dry it properly with a towel. Evidently it was too tight for much air to get in because, for an amazingly long time, little drops seemed to ooze out from beneath it, down my neck, onto the tee-shirt I wore in bed in the summer to protect me from the air-conditioning. I waited to turn the latter on until the water had evaporated completely from the collar, but as I waited I fell asleep. I awoke in the dark, feeling feverish and unpleasant, the collar still wet – this time from my sweat.

What if I have an allergic reaction to the metal? What if I get a strep throat? asthma? My throat was swore and swollen, I had trouble breathing. I took a Valium, and, while waiting for it to work, another.

Thinking of all the ways I might choke to death, I had, as you might imagine, an uneasy sleep, during which I resolved that, despite the consequences I would have the collar removed by a jeweler first thing in the morning.

4.
Commitment

50

Of course I did not.

Now we come to the heart of the story, where things are no longer led up to but transpire, where Fantasies end and Action begins, where the titillations of delay and suspense give way to the supposed pleasures of fulfillment. I am talking as much about esthetic satisfaction as I am about orgasm. Indeed, what is the difference, save one favors the Body and the other the Mind?

You remember, being a child, the story read to you. A little older and you turn the pages. You are lying on a bed in the attic in the sun. The dust motes float softly through the air, and you wonder why, save these moments in the attic, you don't see them. Maybe you move too quickly. Slow down then, for surely they are always there; they don't surround you only when you read. Like tiny snow they drift upon your head, the air is hushed and hot and making you sleepy but you cannot bear to put the book down. But if you don't put it down, look what happens, you'll only have to start another....

Do you want this book to end, so you can start a new one? Are you scared for this book to end, because you must start a new one? There is nothing I can tell you. Anything I know is already known, by you, whether or not you know you know. You want to lie there in the sun, turning the pages, as dinner goes uncooked, the children are fighting, your voice on the phone machine tells the world you are not there....

You are not there. You are here, with me, in this room, the room I share with her, the *rooms* I share with her, during this strange summer. Two rooms, really, mine and hers. Mine is big and white and looks upon the river, a soothing view until you realize those are helicopters over there and airplanes against the red sky, the city of the future as depicted in movies. It is a beautifully proportioned room so soothing to the eye that often in the middle of the day I lie on the bed that juts out from the wall like a gigantic shelf (platform recessed underneath), no other furniture visible, but the beauty of its view can terrorize, especially toward sunset. Hers is a beige room (I imagine), once white but drained of brightness and hue due to time and traffic and over-cooked meat and the disincentive of rent control laws on the improvement of apartments, and there are other rooms too, in one of which an oversized canine sleeps. It is a nondescript building of the kind you probably know, reddish brown stone, or maybe beige brick, in a neighborhood so ancient and uncared for that its very ugliness has rendered it chic and therefore more expensive than it ought to be. Still, it is not expensive – not what people on my side of town think expensive. You climb the stairs, there is no dishwasher or clothes dryer, but it is not difficult or even unpleasant to live here, not at all, the very shabbiness embraces you in your failures. Even the neighbors.... When the sun goes down you may not notice it, because you are not facing west, and the yellow of the streetlight replaces the pink of the sky so it takes awhile to notice the slight diminishment of hue and the settling in of night, the domestic sounds of Spanish overlapping. Just as well perhaps you don't really understand – though most, sometimes all, the words are familiar – it soothes you in the way lullabies do a child who cannot sleep, reminding you of drowsy holidays in warm places with lots of sand and coconuts. How can anything horrible happen when Spanish is being spoken? Yet the pistol rings out in the night....

And as you lie on the bed, as you turn the pages, as your life goes on hold (but how pleasant to hear sounds from far away: the radio, the helicopters, the children playing) – what are you looking for, dear Reader, so supine and passive in my hands?

51

"Because you are my slave, all that you do or do not do must be done – or undone, not in relation to yourself, but to me. Whether in my presence or my absence makes no difference. In fact, *especially* in my absence, where it is up to you and you alone to bear the responsibility of your word. You are to obtain a new mobile phone with a number no one shall know but me. This phone will have only one purpose: to connect us with an umbilical cord that obviates the only *apparent* spatial separation (for we will be as close as if we lived in the same room – no, *closer*) between us. Each call must be answered by the third ring; a busy signal or No Answer will be greeted by the direst of consequences.

"Each morning you must await my orders, wherein you will learn what is required and forbidden for that day. Sometimes these will be in the form of punishments for transgressions you have confided to me – as you *will* (though you chortle to yourself you will not). Often, in fact, you will commit them merely for the purpose of confessing them to me; other times they will be in response to transgressions which I have discovered in some other fashion" (but how? I felt a thrill), "for which the punishment, of course, is more severe. Occasionally my commands will seem incomprehensible, the stuff of nightmares. But they are at the heart of our relationship – the real stuff for which the superficialities of externals" (she flicked my back with a whip) "are merely the signifiers. Pain is not the end, it is merely the tool, and the acquiescence of the heart – the *joyful* acquiescence of the heart – is of far greater significance than of the body.

"But as it is the body which is visible, so too must be those actions that connote the meaning and shape of your mind and your heart. And your body, for the length of the contract, is no longer yours. It is mine, at least within the rules allowed by our 'game.' Do you have any idea what these rules might be?"

"Fidelity?"

"Faithfulness, of course, is required, which includes total abstention from any sexual act that takes place not in my pres- ence – by which I include masturbatory actions or even fantasies. But that is so obvious as to be scarcely worth mentioning. In fact, that diminishes our relationship by implying that what goes on between us is merely sexual. Or rather, for I do not mean to diminish the word 'sexual,' let me say that the erotic extends far beyond what it is ordinarily implied by that word. Indeed, during the course of our relationship you will discover that there is nothing that is not erotic – or at least 'eroticizable' – by the attention you and I will devote to it. If, for instance, I tell you you must not under any circumstances turn on the cold water faucet in your bathroom sink, will not the silver color of the spigot – I assume it is silver, Chris, and not porcelain or gold?" (I nodded) – "glow ever more brightly, until you can scarcely refrain from touching it. And you'll feel this way, not only when you're in the bathroom, but in the furthest corner of your apartment. Even on the street, perhaps, you'll think of it, and have to go home and surreptitiously enter the darkened room and stand, hand extended, almost touching, so close you can feel the pull of the electrons on your hairs, those pads of callused skin at the end of your fingers grow warm from the molecules dancing, pulling, seducing, glowing in the light of the bathroom until you can stand it no longer, you stick out your pinkie, a flash goes through you – the cold but lightning hot flash of the obscene, forbidden, overwhelmingly desired object.... Dare you pretend that the satisfaction you get from this illicit caress differs in any significant degree from that which you get when your fluids gush to drown my fingers, when your ass rises in the air to receive the caresses of the paddle, or when I press my fingers against your Adam's apple....

"You will soon see, if you don't already, but I am certain you must at least *suspect* (for surely this is why you sought me out – not so much to provide what you want, but to affirm what you already know but are too afraid to acknowledge) that we live, not in our bodies but our minds, and your sufferings are neither ordained nor necessary. And the stricter I become, the more exacting my standards, the more constrained your activities, the more fulfilled you will become. Everyday life will begin to seem like a dream in which every gesture possesses a hidden meaning, every sensation a reminder of what happens in these rooms, every thought a paraphrase of the relations between us, as if the external world were but the Platonic shadow of this Ideal. And the more fulfilled you become the more you will crave this, so that, in your obsessive and claustrophobic gluttony you will incessantly demand further and further refinements of my initial instructions, until finally, whereas Orthodox Jews have, I believe, some 613 laws which must be obeyed, you will have 900, nay, 1350, till every breath, every inhalation and exhalation, and the

pause in-between, shall in some sense be a 'signifier' of me –
well, not of 'me,' for in a sense I myself am nothing – but the tool
through which you will achieve that transcendence you have not
yet been able to find. Exhausting, really, to me. But the peculiar
'bond' we have created between us…."

I was as struck by the words 'signifier' and 'transcendence'
as I was by the content of what she said. Indeed, I could scarcely
believe my ears, for in the narrative I had constructed of her she
was – albeit possessing some amount of native intelligence or
instinct – 'uneducated': i.e., had received her degree at one of
the city or state colleges. I am not, believe me, unnecessarily
demeaning the public university system, but only acknowledging
such outrages as I have witnessed – perhaps even helped per-
petrate – firsthand.

"What are you thinking?" she suddenly asked.

"It sounds absurd, but I was wondering if you went to … a
decent college."

"What do you mean by a 'decent' college?"

"An Ivy League school, or at least an Ivy League type school,
like Michigan or Stanford. Or even someplace like Bard."

"'Even someplace like Bard!' The rest are no good?"

"Not 'no good.' But—"

"But what—?"

"I'd be more comfortable if—"

"If I went to a school like one you went to?"

"Yes."

"Why?"

"Because I'd know you were educated."

"You don't think I'm educated?"

"Well – not until you mentioned Plato."

"That impressed you?"

"Not impressed. *Surprised*. Also your use of such words as—"

"—as 'signifier' and 'transcendence'?"

"Yes."

"Why were you surprised?"

"Because ... because ...."

"Do you think only people who went to 'Ivy League type schools' have heard of Plato?"

"Of course not."

"Do you think that someone who read *The Village Voice* for a week couldn't give you a definition of 'signifier'?"

"Not surprised. *Relieved*."

"Relieved because I read *The Village Voice* at least once?"

"No! Because if I could be sure you knew what signifier meant, then I'd know that ... this ... has meaning."

"Does *this* have meaning?" She put what felt like the edge of a knife to my lip and sliced it. Salty liquid slid down my lip into my mouth.

"I don't know."

"You mean, this only has meaning if I went to someplace like Harvard? But if I went to a city college, or – worse – a *community* college, or – god forbid! – *no college at all!* – it would have no meaning?"

Either she was *very* intelligent and was posing a koan, or she was a fool with the standard reply.

Either I was intelligent, not answering that for which there was no answer, or I was a simpleton, for (not) doing the same.

She could easily prove she was intelligent, by saying: 'stop demanding that the world ratify your judgments.'

Or she could say: 'this has nothing to do with intelligence, only about your desire to obfuscate your embarrassing need for submission.'

Or she could even say: 'this has nothing to do with intelligence, only about *my* desire to obfuscate *my* embarrassing need for power....'

But why should she say anything, since I would stay there anyway?

"I wasn't trying to insult you. It's just you asked what was going on in my head."

"And who decides what goes on in your head?"

"Not me. If I did, I would never be unhappy or lonely or wrong."

"But you *want* to be. That's the only thing that makes you real. So if I—"

This time she put the knife against the artery at the side of my neck, then paused, and in the silence after her suspended movement this is what I imagined she thought: that if I were never lonely or unhappy I would not be a masochist, and if I were not a masochist I would not be here, and if I were not here this dance of pleasure we were commencing would not be ours. And the reason she stopped her hand was one, to remind me what the world would be like were I not here, and two, to prove that I could not dictate her actions, even by my mini-rebellions of behavior or thought.

"It is *impossible* for you to insult me, Chris," she said. "You are the one tied up and blindfolded, and it is me you have come to for instruction and refinement. Your verbal rebellions are pathetic, but typical of one in your position. I permit them, when I do, solely for my own amusement."

She pressed the knife, but on its side, so it could not cut, and I let go, relaxing into a combo of happiness and fatigue, even as I still yearned to know if she had gone to college, and if so, *where?* And the tears trickled out from my eyes, as we began to discuss the 1350 refinements she had alluded to earlier.

She wanted me to name them. I did not.

The knife pressed into my throat. My head bowed, mumbling, I began to name all the things she might choose to have me do or not do: "eat, drink, talk on the telephone, take a bath, meet friends, go to the health club, piss, shit, do laundry, buy toilet paper...."

"Louder."

"....iron, wash the floor, read a book, brush my teeth, floss, put moisturizer on my face, drink alcohol, beer, wine, coke, play the tv or radio, turn the light on, off, middle...." And thus, as night turned into day, or vice versa (since I had no sense of what time it was), I enumerated the 1800 rules of which she had spoken, until there was nothing – no action, no gesture, no thought – which did not have relevance to this strange game we were playing. And when I did what I should, I would be praised, and when I failed, as surely I would, I would be punished, so that all aspects of my life would be suffused with meaning, even those in which I performed the most mundane of chores. I tried to remember the last time anyone had cared, *really cared*, about what I did or did not do, and I couldn't....

52

I lie on the bed, nipple clamps on my breast. Original scheduled time one hour, but each time they slip off the time is extended by thirty minutes.

As my cooperation is unverifiable, I commence the activity in a purely experimental mode, fully intending to release myself when the duration seems sufficient to be able to plausibly describe the experience to her. In the absence of her coolly articulated commands, her flicks and blows, her approvals and reprimands – what pleasure can there be save that of the purely conceptual?

(Not to say that many of the pleasures in her presence are not also conceptual!)

Yet when she calls to release me the clamps are still on my nipples. Hours have, in fact, gone by. I am unable to answer on the required number of rings, as any quick repositioning of my body will cause the clamps to slip and further extend my punishment, so either way I deserve more punishment.

To my surprise, she grants me amnesty. I am, almost, sorry. The enforced stillness, the numbness of the sensation on my nipples, the knowledge of the excruciating pain I will experience when I release them – but most of all, the fact that we are doing this for *me* – makes a beautiful counterpoint of absence and presence that both acknowledges and pacifies the Void.

53

I spend a day completely naked. Someone buzzes with a delivery, but I must tell him to leave the package outside the door, and pick it up only when the elevator has gone. I lie on the bed, my legs apart, sun dancing on the seahorses behind my lids, yearning to touch myself. I don't.

54

The day I am forbidden to stand, but must crawl around the apartment on my knees, the sky is white with heat. The sweat on my knees and hands soaks up the dirt from the floor, and I abandon all attempts to remain fastidious, lying on my side even in dust. For the first few hours I carry my food and water bowls with me as I move around the loft, to guard them from Esmeralda, but the more I protect them the more interested she becomes, until in an unwitting moment I catch her drinking from my bowl. I quickly finish the food. Somewhere in what, by the angle of the sun I assume is the afternoon (no watch is permitted, and all clock faces have been turned against the wall), thirst overcomes me and I lower myself toward the water. It looks okay, normal, save for some dust floating on the surface, but in fact there is an acrid smell, that I can only imagine comes from Esmeralda's saliva. I drink from it anyway.

55

I am on the floor, one hand cuffed to the radiator, a cooler of food and water and a green plastic pail beside me, forbidden to read, watch television, listen to music, talk on the phone until the phone call announcing my liberation comes.

Initially, I am merely bored. I fight the impulse to sleep – an activity strictly forbidden, as it would remove my awareness from my bondage, for I am to remain completely conscious of my servitude, my utter dependence on her orders – all the more poignant for being so apparently purposeless.

But soon, the discomfort (from the handcuffed wrist) and the pain (from same) take over my consciousness: so many knobby parts that touch the floor with more pressure or less cushioning of fat than others. To name some: shoulder, shoulder blades, elbows, ankle bones, back of head, wrists, side of hand, back of arm, fingertips, hip, coccyx, ass, knee, thigh, back.... I rotate these parts in turn against the floor, pressing down, then releasing, as if massaging them, but just as one part relaxes and is able to touch the floor, another begins to bear pressure, so that no matter what position I roll into, I am unable to stay still for long, as at night in insomnia one constantly turns toward and away from the person in bed with one, a fitting objective correlative for the endless cycle of acceptance and rejection....

What this has to do with sex I don't know. Then why was I wet?

My greatest fear while undergoing my trials was that she would utterly forget I was performing them, and thus fail to release me (and that, while waiting, I would pass out and die), or, even if she remembered in time, was not conscious *each and every second* of the pain I was undergoing (which of course she could not be).

But without her awareness, what meaning did any of this have?

To be precise, the meaning resided in my consciousness of *her* consciousness.

If she did not call, however, might it not mean that she had not forgotten, but had merely changed the rules of the game?

Perhaps there were no rules, only an ever-changing process so subtle that articulation of the rules itself changed the game, as in quantum mechanics or Russell's Theory of Types. Or, perhaps, the *discovery* of the rules (as illustrated by one's correct antici-pation of future moves) was *itself* the game – only part of this game *included the concealment from one's partner that one had discovered the rules*. Perhaps it was necessary to deny there was a game at all, even at moments of so-called 'greatest intimacy.' And how was one to win the game? The persona one adopts for playing the game ('courtesan,' 'vampire,' 'ice princess,' etc.) should remain as co-terminus with one's 'real self' as possible (the repertoire of moves being far more devel-oped, of course, for such a persona than any other), so that its artifice would remain almost impossible to divine (and not just by one's opponent – but *oneself!* For to fool oneself was surely the greatest and most difficult trick of all....)

The point of the Game comes when by adroit anticipation of the Other's reactions to one's moves, one successfully manipu-lates the Other into the utterance of the words: "I love you."

The chance to play the game, alas, decreases as one grows older, as the business of life becomes ever more complex and demanding, and because, as by that point only the most refined and complicated version will suffice to retain interest, it becomes increasingly difficult to find an experienced and attractive com-petitor willing to devote the time and labor to competing at the level one requires. Which is why, I suppose, one sultry June morning I succumbed to the allure of a newspaper advertise-ment....

As the phone continued not to ring (a quantum-type nonevent that 'occurs' *only* in its articulation), I had ample time to philoso-phize about such games in general and our own in particular, and soon anxiety about my digestive processes replaced both boredom and discomfort as my major concern.

I had determined to end this particular game before it was time to use that green plastic pail, yet at some point in the early afternoon I found myself crouching over it, in a position made incredibly awkward due to the necessity of keeping the hand-cuffed wrist in close proximity to the radiator. The sun through the windows and the dehumidifying aspect of the air-conditioning quickly dried my excretions, but long before this I had become accustomed to (and thus was unable to notice) the smell. Nonetheless, during the course of the day and night and part of the next day (she did not telephone for an extremely long period of time, during which I became convinced not just that she forgotten me but that she had devised this task as a way of terminating the relationship), the contents of the pail – earthy, materialistic – came to seem emblematic of my being.

Was her awareness of these metaphorical possibilities the impetus for this particular command?

Meanwhile time passed, the sky grew dark, I looked at it like a nun from a convent cell, the slight lightening of the deep blue as dawn approached. No, not dawn, the moon, encircled by a halo the diameter of which (counting both sides) might also be as wide as the moon, but far paler. I began to see colors in this halo, pale rainbow tints that one could only see if one were patient, and which I decided were reward for my endurance of my sufferings.

At some point, naturally, I did fall asleep (although only for the briefest of moments), which necessitated, two days later, my being forced to spend a number of hours naked on my bed with my ass in the air.

56

All the anxiety is in the original choice. Once past the initial humiliation, once shame is accepted, once one ceases to struggle, life becomes oddly relaxing. I grow accustomed to days passing almost without notice, with little happening save my lying on my bed with my eyes closed, imagining I was in the room with her, imagining I was at my health club swimming, imagining I was talking to Leslie about her.

"What does she look like?"

"I don't know."

"What's her name?"

"I don't know."

"Are you crazy?"

"I don't know."

I pick up the straw (I am drinking an ice cream soda) and blow chocolate-flavored seltzer at Leslie. She pretends to be irritated, but she is amused.

The phone rings. It is Leslie. I don't answer.

57

"Have you disobeyed me since you were last here?" she asked.

"Yes sir!"

"And what is it you did?"

"I touched myself," I said.

"Where?"

"My vagina."

"Where, precisely?"

"The labia."

"For how long?"

"Just a few minutes."

"How long are a 'few'?"

"Three, perhaps."

"You were looking at your watch?"

"No."

"So it could have been longer?"

"Maybe." Smack. "Yes."

"Did you enjoy it?"

"Not really."

"So you didn't get wet at all?"

"A little, maybe." Smack.

"What else?"

"I ate ice cream without permission."

Smack. "What else?"

"I watched tv. A baseball game."

"An *entire* game?"

"No. Well, almost all."

"Several hours, you mean."

"I didn't mean to. But I turned it on without thinking, and once I started watching, I knew I'd get punished anyway."

"Did you think you'd be punished the same amount for doing something without thinking as perpetuating such a mistake consciously?"

"I suppose."

"And what do you think would be a proper punishment for turning on the tv 'without thinking,' as you put it?"

"Twenty strokes?" I volunteered. She was silent. "Thirty? Fifty? A hundred?"

"And for continuing when you knew you shouldn't?"

"A stroke per minute – not counting the original ones?"

"How many minutes?"

"About an hour," I said.

"Maybe a little longer?"

"Maybe."

"75 strokes, plus 100, 175. Is that fair?"

"Pretty fair," I said.

"Maybe a bit longer?"

"Maybe."

"200 strokes. Do you think you can handle that, Chris?"

"Of course."

"You sound confident."

I shrugged.

"Even like you're looking forward to it?"

"Not exactly."

"But a little?"

"I'm . . . curious," I admitted.

"Is that why you left the tv on, Chris, because you wanted me to hit you for an exceedingly long period of time?"

"No."

"Your mother didn't spank you enough, Chris. We all know that." She paused. "But I'm not your mother."

As she talked, she had lifted my arms, and attached them to something above my head and slightly apart, so that I had to stand slightly on tiptoe so as not to have my arms pull on my sockets. There was silence, then an enormous whack.

"Ow!" I screamed, in surprise as well as pain.

"I think you've been laboring under a misapprehension, Chris. Perhaps you thought I was going to paddle you, or whip you. But do you know what this is?" And she struck me again.

"A cane?" I asked, when I recovered my breath.

"*Very* good!" And she hit me again. "You've never been hit 200 times with a cane, have you Chris?"

I gasped. "No."

"I've hardly hit you at all with a cane, have I?"

"I don't think so."

"I know so. You'd remember. It makes nice little stripes, and they don't disappear in a day or two either."

"*Ow!*"

"I've hit you, what is it? 4 times? But 200 is fair?"

"I guess that's what I said."

"What about 250?"

"I spose."

"300?"

I wondered how long this game would go. "That sounds like a lot. What if I pass out from the pain?"

"Then you won't feel it."

"Couldn't that seriously injure me?"

"I don't know. I'm not sure if I've ever caned anyone that much before. Maybe next time you'll pay a little more attention to the rules."

"I do. *Oww.*"

"Surely you turned the tv off after the baseball game?" I was silent.

"*Ow.* Maybe a few more minutes. *Ow.* I'm sorry."

"Sorry *what*?"

"Sorry, *sir. Ow!!!*"

"I don't think you're sorry. I think you just did this to see how far you can go. You like to see how far you can go, don't you?"

"No. *Ow.* Are these counting against the total?" I asked.

"Until you asked if they were."

"That's not fair!" Already my back was soaked with sweat.

"This is not about fairness." She hit me again.

"Stop!" I screamed.

"You know the safe word. If you want me to stop, use it."

Then it really began, by far the most intense and extensive pain I had ever experienced from her. Initially I felt it outside, as a kind of excruciating but limited sharpness on the skin, then as a deeper, under-the-skin pain (though one still limited to the butt and thigh area), then it spread everywhere, so even my nipples and the tips of my fingers began to ache. My jaw hurt too, from clenching, and I had to choose between easing my toes – sore and numb from standing on tiptoe – or my arms and shoulders, which, when I relaxed my feet, felt like they were being wrenched from my body. I tried to rotate my torso or raise or lower my body a few millimeters so that I could vary the precise placement of her blows, but she caught onto this and waited for me to shift into the position she wanted. In any case, after a short while the fatigue from pain and from holding myself up began to take over, and I hung there, my legs buckling, my arms raw, as she struck my ass, legs, back, and thighs.

As always, when being punished, I squeezed my eyes tightly, as if to hide myself from myself, and as always I felt like an astronaut hurtling silently through space. With each stroke I would seem to float away from my body, then the stroke would bring me back in for a second, then I'd float away again, and this rhythm itself was comforting, and my body gradually became numb, and the numbers ticked away.

At 64, she suddenly stopped. I felt almost . . . disappointed.

"I can take more," I told her.

"It's not *you* I'm worried about, but the neighbors. You're screaming."

"Am I?"

"I'm going to have to gag you."

A pause. "You have my permission," I said.

"What about the code words?"

"I won't need them."

"Are you sure?"

"Yes."

I opened my mouth, and she stuffed what I assumed (from its smell and texture) was an athletic sock in my mouth.

Every ten strokes or so, she would stop to see if I were all right, or if I wanted her to stop. I'd shake my head, and the strokes would again begin.

But each time more slowly, and with less force. Finally she stopped and took the sock out of my mouth. "Red code, Chris," she said. "Please."

I couldn't talk, but I shook my head 'no.'

She replaced the sock in my mouth, and began swinging with more force. The pain was so great it was no longer pain, but the world. I tried to hide in a little corner of it, a tiny little corner where I wouldn't be noticed and could think of something else.

Eventually, for perhaps only a second, I blacked out. When I woke up, I wasn't being hit, and there was an incredible silence. A silence of car sounds and Charlie and even the blood pounding through my body, but still, somehow, silence.

"You win," I heard.

She put her arms around me and held me up like a puppet

as first one hand, then the other, was released. I collapsed on the floor.

I opened my mouth, but the sock hung there, stuck in my dry mouth. She pulled it out and handed me a glass of water. I drank it, greedily but carefully, afraid of sucking it into my lungs in my eagerness, and when I was done she handed me another.

"I'm sorry about the gag. I enjoy hearing your screams."

"I like you to hear them," I managed to say. "I wish you could."

"We could. Far away. A cabin in the woods. Would you like that?"

Pause. "Sure. Why not?"

"Anything could happen in a place like that."

"Yes."

"Of course, anything could happen here too."

"Yes."

She helped me to my feet and led me down the hall ("shh, Charlie," I could hear him sigh and resettle himself as we moved past) to a place of cold floor and walls. She helped me into the tub. The cool of the porcelain soothed my body. "Lie down," she ordered. She squatted over me. I could feel the warm liquid dripping onto my skin. She rubbed into my body with hers, dampening me with a combination of sweat and pee.

Then she moved her body up, over my chin. "Open your mouth."

I turned my head, but she held it still and opened it.

I felt the warm trickle landing on my tongue, sliding down the back of my teeth. I lifted my tongue to block the entrance to my throat so the pee sat in a kind of little puddle in my lower jaw. I smelled nothing, as the position of my tongue blocked the passage to my nasal receptors, but I could taste the salt and feel the warmth.

She squirted a little more, and the residue began to spill over my lips and down my chin. It tickled.

"You don't want to waste my golden elixir, do you?" she asked.

I shook my head. "No." It sounded like a gargle.

"So swallow."

She forced my mouth open even more, so that to prevent myself from drowning I had to swallow. The saltiness tickled, and I swallowed again to soothe it. Each time my mouth was empty she peed a little more, and each time I swallowed it.

It was less unpleasant than you would have thought.

After the last drops had trickled down, she lowered herself onto my mouth, so I could lick the residue of urine from her pubic hair and lips.

"You *are* a good girl, Chris," she said.

I felt pleased, like I had won a prize in school. Then I passed out.

58

She's a director, of course, shooting a movie. Later I will get paid, and become an underground star.

Actually, I'm an actress, only I've been programmed to forget this so I can play my part more authentically. They've made me think I'm a writer. They've made me think I'm living with someone who's currently in Sweden, but I'm really living with her.

Actually, she's the Current, playing an elaborate extended joke, to demonstrate once and for all that she is not (as she insists I believe) lacking in imagination, intelligence, and wit. Not to mention deviousness and perversity. She is doing this to make me fall madly in love with her, at which point she will leave me. At which point I will admire her all the more.

It's not the Current after all, but the one before the one before the Current. They're so alike I get them confused. She's mad about something that happened ten years ago, I can no longer remember what. But she thinks about it every day....

Actually, it's that fat person I once let fuck me at a party, I can tell by the touch. Took forever to live it down. She kept calling but I never picked up the phone. She's getting her revenge.

It's the Black Panthers, in an elaborate payback for some heedless remark I made once about affirmative action.

It's Sex Panic, on a dare by Larry Kramer.

No, it's some guy I once let fuck me. He had a very tiny dick. "Is that all there is?" I said without thinking. He's been waiting for this his entire life.

No, it's a fellow writer. A female fellow writer. The one whose books get compared unfavorably to mine. "A second-rate ____," they say. But she's learning my tricks. She's fucking with my head and she's fucking my head. If she's still second-rate, it won't be my fault.

59

I'm in a chair with my legs strapped to its legs and my arms fastened behind, a huge box-like contraption on my shoulders. The box prevents me from turning my head, and functions as blinders, eliminating any peripheral vision. Her fingers fumble at my face, pull off the blindfold. For the first time in her presence, my eyes are open. I can see nothing, for the light seems over-whelming, a screen in front of me glows.

Sound comes, then a picture. It's tv. Midnight Blue. Two girls licking the nipples of a third. Call 1-900-B-R-E-A-S-T-S. A man lies on the bed as one girl gives him a blow job and the other licks his balls. 1-900-S-U-C-K-I-N-G. An Asian girl opens her mouth to drink water, no it's piss. 1-900-S-H-O-W-E-R-S. Guys flex serious biceps, sweat – 1-900-J-O-C-K-G-Y-M. A girl kneels on the carpet, her back to the camera, hands tied behind her back. Close-ups of her neck, hands placing something on it, a collar. Similar to mine. No. Identical. Camera pulls back, neck, shoulders, dark hair like me, quick shot of a girl on bed, immedi-ate CU butt twitching, as the paddle SMACKS! Loudly, again and again, CU cheeks spread as the silicone mold of the male member, dripping with lube, enters, lips are opened, CU hair all wet and gooey, from lube or otherwise, the barking of a dog....

Curse, scream, howls. I'm an actress, and I don't like it. Fingers in my face, I bite, scream, fingers force open my teeth, she tries to shove what feels like a ball in my mouth. I clamp teeth. She pinches my nostrils. With the muscles of my nose I try to push them apart, with the muscles of my nose I widen the bottoms, but no match for her. I curl my lips up, try to suck air in through teeth, but her hand goes over my mouth, and while the blackness approaches, I open my mouth.

The ball gag is so large it barely fits in my mouth.

She tells me she's been taping me all along. Moi the movie star, the whole shebang, on tape. "You remember, Chris, don't you? *If you break the contract, I no longer respect the privacy of our agreement.*"

What could be more predictable? Nonetheless, I start to retch. The ball is pulled out, lest I choke on the vomit. I'm coughing, choking, the way you do when there's not enough saliva to cough with, and though there's no saliva, I feel like drowning. I gasp wildly, so the sounds of hoarseness will cover up fear. The tv goes off.

"You didn't suspect?"

I try to speak, but mouth so dry from ball, no sound. Breathe through mouth, makes drier. "Water," I try to say, "water," but it's a whisper, a croak, because of the dryness. "Waa" – a baby crying. "Waa waa" – a little girl crying, in an empty room, long ago.

"Would you like water?" I cough, nod. "Then stay still." I let her reattach the blindfold, and she gives me a glass of water.

"You should thank me for immortalizing you. What film star has ever been so open, so poignant, so giving of herself? Forever you will be lowering your head to the collar, forever you will be hoisting your ass in the air, forever you will be gratefully receiving my strokes . . . and, if not *exactly young*, than at least no older than you are now. You'll beg me to show it to my friends. Not just my friends – *your* friends – Midnight Blue – so all the world can know you as you really are. No one does, do they? It's lonely. You tell them the false secrets and they think they're the real secrets so you have contempt for them . . . . You've even told your girlfriend and still she has *no idea.* And not just her, your *mother* – she never knew you either . . . nor your father . . . . Nobody has the slightest . . . . But maybe it's just as well, because who would love you if they did, you're such a disgusting creature? When you come right down to it, probably nobody has ever really loved you . . . I mean, *really* loved you . . . for who you were and not who they pretended you were. Sad, isn't it? terribly terribly sad . . . the saddest thing really...because that's all you ever wanted...and that's what you never got...until now...."

"You promised me privacy. How do I know you're not... showing it ...somebody?" I managed to gasp.

"You'll just have to trust me." I moan. "If you don't trust me, what are you doing with your life in my hands? I could kill you, and no one would ever know."

"I've left your address in my house."

"You don't *really* think this is my apartment, do you?"

"Fingerprints—"

She laughs.

"God forgive me. I mean *you*."

Her hands again around my neck. Harder and harder she squeezes. I tighten the muscles, sinews, tendons, whatever, as much as I can, but of course she is stronger. She's right, I was stupid to trust her, she's right to kill me, for my stupidity and trust. People like me deserve to killed, *are* killed, every day, all over the world. This logic calms me, so I let go, relax, soothing really, not so bad...no more struggles, here or anywhere, no mail, no calls, no bills, no papers, there's the white light....

60

Home, an indeterminate time later, I examine myself in the mirror. To the 'naked' eye, of course, I am the person in the video, but really I am someone else, someone who has never been in that apartment, or even in my loft, but someone else entirely, who lives in another place. I don't know where, exactly, though I've searched for it my entire life. Nonetheless, that life is my real life, the one I am meant to be living, and this one – with a career I have grown indifferent to and a roommate who is a stranger and objects I do not need – is the imitation. And if this is the imitation, the life I lead with the one I do not know who does things to me in an apartment I have never seen is the dream. I prefer the dream to the imitation but neither is real, and I feel cheated because I know I will never really live my life, my real life.

Truly, who would even recognize this shell of a person who does not even share my body but walks a few inches ahead of me, transparent and slightly to the left?

61

The Current calls. It's been a long time since I have turned on my computer, let alone tried to e-mail. I listen to her voice for a while before I can figure out who she is, this stranger talking to me as if she knows me, whose voice is unfamiliar, whose intonations I don't recognize, whose smell I don't remember, who talks of events that have the deadened but over-detailed quality of implanted memories. It's a desultory conversation, mostly about finances and Esmeralda. Without warning, as I am describing how Esmeralda tormented a fly the other night, she hangs up.

This counterpoints the unspoken narrative, in which I do not love her enough (and never will, because that's who I am) and she loves me too much (that's who she is).

This narrative has nothing to do with reality, but everything to do with truth. In reality the Current will leave, as she always does, when she finds someone whom she can more plausibly believe will love her forever. In reality I will be left, as I always am. It serves me right, not for what I do or do not do, but who I am.

62

"I need to be punished, sir," I said. I saluted and stood at attention, my chest puffed way out, my hand at my brow.

"Why is that?"

"Because I have disobeyed orders."

"Which of my commands have you broken?"

"The bathroom command, sir. The asking of permission re. watching of tv and answering of telephones. I even began to suggest a hint of our secret pact to Alice—"

"Who's Alice?"

"She lives in California, sir. She won't betray my confidence. I needed to talk to somebody."

"We never know where our enemies reside. Any other broken commands, soldier?"

"Yes sir."

"What are they?"

"I don't remember. But I'm sure there are many."

"At ease."

"Thank you sir."

I ended the salute, put my hands behind my back, and spread my legs.

"Do you understand what war is, soldier?" she demanded.

"Yes sir."

"And what is that?"

"Total commitment, a willingness to sacrifice oneself for

one's comrades, commander, and the cause, ending only in achievement of goals or death."

"Have you done your part as well as you could – not just today but in general?"

"No, sir."

"And why is that?"

"Because I am lazy and unworthy."

"Why is that?"

"Bad upbringing."

"Many people have upbringings involving far greater abuse and deprivation than yours, indeed are raised with scarcely an upbringing at all, yet they are not necessarily as lazy and unwilling as you are."

"I was about to add, sir, that I have a bad character."

"And who is responsible for your bad character?"

"Although part of the component is doubtless genetic, and other habits were inculcated at an early age, I am of course responsible for my behavior, as there are offsprings of psychopaths and sociopaths who make fine members of the community, sir."

"Very good. Acknowledgment of responsibility is the first step toward becoming an autonomous being."

"Thank you, sir, for the compliment. But I have far to go."

"That's true. But this indication of responsibility indicates you are perhaps ready for more advanced training."

"How so?"

"You will, starting now, become responsible for administering punishments for those transgressions you commit when not in my presence. You will administer them in the same degree and spirit as I would, so that you become a stand-in for me. It will be done as follows. You will keep a list of those things you did not do that you were supposed to, and those you did that you were not supposed to, and even those in which your performance was rather indifferent. At the end of each day you will look at this list and determine what the appropriate response should be – that is, what I myself would advocate – and perform it. Do you understand?"

"Yes sir."

"You will, from time to time, report these infractions and the punishments you have chosen to me. Naturally, the administration of insufficient punishment will itself be punished by a punishment."

"Naturally."

She laid out, in great detail, other instructions also, which equally excited and repelled me. Then I confessed my offenses since my previous visit, and suggested appropriate punishments, of which she approved. She said I had repaid her belief in my integrity and honesty, and commanded me to go home and administer these to myself.

I begged her to change her mind. "It will not have the same effect if I do it to myself."

"Why not?"

"The lack of your enjoyment of my pain will diminish the effect of the punishment."

"On the contrary. My enjoyment of your debasement diminishes the pain, so my absence will only serve to increase it. But that is not entirely true either, for of course you will hold my existence within your head, so that in all relevant ways I will still be in the room with you."

63

When asked how I had done, the next time I saw her, I said I
had taken her lessons to heart, and explained to her all that
had transpired. She told me she approved of my decisions, and
rewarded me by a spanking from her own hand, which, as I
knew from experience, hurt her more than it did me.

64

Her concern re. my disobeying for the sake of being punished
turned out to be in vain. For, as much as I craved punishments
when administered by her hand, I discovered I craved the
pleasure of her approval even more. In my mind, also, I found
myself in competition with my fellow 'soldiers,' and naturally
I wanted to be the best, so that, when our relationship should
end, she would share in at least some of my bereavement.

65

We are held together not by meetings, but by the orders that
bind us. For, after all, how often do I see her? Once or twice
a week? Rarely more, and sometimes less. It has been raining
heavily for days, and all this time I have not heard from her. I
spend my time lying in bed or staring out at the window, and eat
an inordinate amount of Chinese food. But that's who's willing
to deliver, even in the rain, cheaply, and with no need for polite
conversation.

66

Sometimes she orders me to talk: streams of words that start out like porno but end up like poems, echolalic convocations of what I am feeling and thinking and what I imagine she is thinking and feeling, what I want her to do to me and what I imagine she wants to do to me, long lists of desires and disappointments, past moments of connection and repulsion: "panting as the giant cock of Charlie enters me, spitting and howling as huge Shepherds take their turn, clanking Germans urinating on the hydrant of my body, sinkholes of the flesh, fetid orifices where late the sweet…."

I am whipped, of course, for my disgusting thoughts.

As the words of every sexual act coveted or feared, every person craved for or loathed, every dialogue dreamed or halluci-nated gets uttered, I become ever emptier and more innocent so that whatever pain and humiliations I undergo are mere asides, inexplicably easy penances for the evil in my soul.

Meanwhile her fist is in my vagina, my tied legs stretched wide like a V, my body numb, sweat long since dried off. I marvel at this place beyond sex, this peace, equal to five Quaaludes, this space where I can never want anything again: through the path of desire I have achieved the space beyond all desire.

Other times, we say almost nothing at all, except maybe a "here's your sock" as I get dressed. Anticipating her every desire, I need no command, only the occasional minor redirection, by the slightest of touches, as if she were a rider and I her horse. Or maybe she makes a sound, as if signaling a dog….

67

I tell her what a wonderful master she is; how firm and in control and considerate she is of me, her slave; that I exist only to do her service; that before her my life was empty, as it will be after; how in her presence I am always wet; how out of her presence I long only to be with her; that I dread the end of summer and the return of the Current; that, could I succumb to my heart's desire, I would remain her slave forever; that I treasure the blue and black flowers she leaves on my skin; that each blow is a caress and each caress a benediction; that I would be ground into dust if she wished it....

In return, am I not the most obedient, the most compliant, the most submissive, the most pliable, the most dutiful, the most malleable, the most receptive, the most persistent, the most loyal, the most diligent, the most deferential, the most dedicated, the most conscientious, the most trustworthy, the most meticulous, the most fastidious, the most industrious, the most painstaking, the most assiduous, the most dependable, the most indefatigable, the most devout etc. slave that has ever or could ever exist on the face of the earth... moon... solar system... galaxy... universe... universes....

I imagine her smiling. I imagine her petting my head.

Is she white, black, Asian? tall or short? thin or fat? young or middle-aged or old? I imagine conversations wherein she confides to me all the secrets of her life: the little country town upstate where she grew up, the gas station her father owned and her brothers worked, how her sisters stuck gum in her hair, how her brother once cut up a frog and left it in her bed, how her mother died young and she had to do the laundry and cooking, how she loved English class and the English teacher, that she pitched on the girls' softball team, that the guidance teacher offered to help get her a scholarship to Vassar but she laughed because none of her friends were into brains, how she made the little girl next door pull down her pants when she was six, how she practiced kissing with her friends on sleepover dates when she was a teenager, that the captain of the football team was in love with her, that she loved marijuana and LSD but hated cocaine, how the father of her best friend stuck his tongue in her mouth one day when he was driving her home after babysitting, how she rode motorcycles and bought her first even before she had her driving permit, how she got in trouble in school because she couldn't keep her mouth shut . . . .

68

An odd encounter at the Korean grocer's, where a woman picks among the cherries with great concentration (oblivious, apparently, to the germs she is leaving for others), as her dog – a breed I don't recognize, with longish unruly hair – utters high-pitched moans and lunges in my direction. Can this be Charlie or am I merely getting my period? The dog seems smaller than I imagine Charlie to be, but I am standing up, and of course Charlie is mythical and monstrous to me, the Beast in *Beauty and the Beast*. I move closer, and he leaps up on me as much as the leash allows.

"Charlie," I say, very softly. He takes no notice of his name, but perhaps he does not hear. He seems happy enough, how-ever, as I stroke his ears.

"AC-DC," the woman says, "stop that."

I stare at the owner, who shows no sign of knowing me, even when I utter Charlie's name again, louder. Then I shut my eyes to remember the sensation of 'Charlie,' who is now attempting to place his paws on my breast.

"I don't know what's the matter with him," she says, jerking at the leash.

"That's okay," I say. "A friend of mine owns a dog like this and we're real good pals."

The false heartiness of this strikes us both at the same time.

"You don't own dogs," the woman replies. "They own you."

I don't know what, if anything, to make of this enigmatic encounter.

69

I am on the floor, kneeling, a latex simulacrum of the male organ in my mouth, my neck stretched back far as it can go. Despite its mammoth proportions (larger than any I remember, whether latex or flesh) it does not repel me with its rubbery texture or alkaline taste, and I ingest it for her, delicately lubricating it with the digestive juices I ordinarily supply her only in kissing, as it slides past barriers of reflex and revulsion to where air and food normally go . . . a diffuse pain that is less a pain than my insides spreading and contracting like the pulse of blood behind the eyelids I am so conscious of lately. Her fingers move around in my mouth, touching my gums in a way that both tickles and makes them a bit numb; she flicks my tongue with her finger, she picks at my teeth with a nail, almost as if removing a morsel

of stuck food. She removes the cock and I feel my throat col-
lapsing, but she replaces it with her fingers, her hand. I stay very
still, breathing softly through the cavities between her fingers.
She begins to spread them, so they touch all parts of my throat
with discrete pressures, like an octopus, which becomes a
complicated rhythm, for, as one finger pulses, another tickles and
a third knocks what feels like a knuckle against the wall of my
throat and also something sharp – a nail maybe – is flicking my
skin. A finger (perhaps from the other hand) is under my tongue,
massaging the strange group of tissues there. Although it is
ticklish and arousing it distracts me from whatever excitement
I was beginning to feel in the throat area, they're too different,
somehow, for me to connect them. But as soon as I switch my
attention from throat to gum, she returns to throat by slightly
increasing first the pressure, then the speed of her fingers, which
makes me want to clear my throat, but also swallow her fingers.
I am confused, and still trying to hold onto the sleepiness of the
tongue and gums. All these transitions are initially merely
annoying, but somehow, between the rhythm and the multitude
of sensations, metamorphose into something enjoyable. Then she
begins to link these for me, by spreading the fingers and massaging the gums so that each movement somehow suggests the
other, like a piece of modern music that starts out with random
sounds but in which a pattern is revealed. And yet her purpose
is not to arouse me, but a demonstration (but to whom?) of
possession, delineating precisely how much an object I am. She
yanks my hair, stretching my neck (pleasant), a third sensation
different enough from the others that it sets up a triangle of
sensations, but one that is confusing: there are too many hands.
I interpret this to mean: *shut up, stop thinking,* give up keeping

track. As always I am frightened of dying, in this case drowning from saliva or choking on vomit – not because she disgusts but because I am not a yogi and the body simply cannot, will not, acquiesce in all our designs. Finally she adds a fourth element, clearly the climax of the "piece" – the curling of her fingers into a fist in my throat. All the energy that has been expended in little jabs and outings coalesces in this central mammoth thrusting. It is difficult to breathe; I also worry she will puncture my insides. But I am happy the further down the fist goes, because for once – *for once* – I am not lonely inside, there where previously only a doctor's hand had been, removing my tonsils.

I want to come, not for myself but for her, as a demonstration of the power she has over me.

If I come desire might end. Then what?

Her hand is in the small of my back, where I could use a massage, and my hairs stand up at attention. I shiver like a little animal.

I have totally forgotten the latex in my ass which has mostly slipped out, the fat part of it resting in the crack. She spreads my cheeks enough so the asshole itself touches the plastic.

She orders me to get on my knees. The dildo still inside, her pulling me by the collar, we go to the bathroom. "Lie on your side," she orders, "with your knees up to your chest."

The dildo comes out and something smaller, slimmer, slips in, something so thin in relation to everything else that I assume it must be some kind of ironic commentary, especially as it tickles when she pushes it. Then there's a pause, some kind of arrangement of something, then a pleasant coolness as water flows in. Enema, I realize, nice and cool. But gradually, behind the coolness, a tingling begins....

She laughs. "Pepper."

The heat overcomes the cold of the water, which also provides an interesting contrast to the cold floor. I twitch. But I'm supposed to lie still and hold it in. It's my order. The pepper gets hotter and hotter.

She helps me into the tub, slowly, carefully, so the liquid stays inside. If it doesn't I must drink it, she tells me, "a nice spicy drink, excellent for the digestion." The night is warm, the tub is cool, inside I am hot; these three temperatures have nothing to do with each other; the hot is more like freezing than warm. Will the pepper burn my insides, or is the word "hot" merely a metaphor? Can one die from this? Has she done this before?

"I am everywhere," she says, "inside and out. I control your bodily functions. You have no powers other than the ones I – temporarily – grant you. You cannot eat, shit, urinate, other than with my permission. You cannot even let anyone else hurt you without my permission. You have no choice in anything. You can't even talk if I don't want you to. Even your little toe" – she brought it, ever so gently, into her mouth, where she bit it – "is utterly at my command. She was stroking my stomach now, off-handedly, terribly softly, and the delicacy – little lines of electricity – worked off the general pain inside so that I was feeling all possible physical sensations (hard soft wet dry warm cold hurt tickle pain arousal), and most of the mental (curiosity, fear, humiliation, submission, desire, love, hate) ones as well. "You'd let me kill you if I wanted to, wouldn't you, Chris?"

I want to say "yes" – not because I wanted to die, but for the thrill of succumbing – of course I don't. "Are you crazy?" I ask.

She laughs. "Don't play stupid. It's what you want. You're just embarrassed to admit it."

"It's not in the contract."

"Contracts can be amended."

Far away (because so much else is happening – my pubic muscles are contracted, my nipples are pinched, a finger slides gently on my clitoris) I hear my voice say "only in a way."

"What way?"

"The...the...." She was alternating ice cubes and little ash burns that supposedly would not permanently mark my body in a hot-cold way that provided an interesting counterpoint to the pepper and the freezing water. Actually, the position I was in bothered me more than the cold and pain. But something was there, beyond the fatigue and the pain, something I am avoiding, a thought that sits there like a file I refuse to open.

What felt like a fingernail made its way over my breast. Perhaps it was a knife. She extended its point to me, and I licked off the salty fluid, not knowing whether it was my blood or hers.

"But if I were dead—"

"Yes?"

"I would not be here."

"Yes?"

"Then...." There was something else, but I could not get to it. Then my mind gave up and my body took over, and what had been inside began exiting, first as a tiny brook but then as a series of expulsions filled with noises and smells. I cannot see it but it is surely brown, the muddy wetness that has begun to slide under my body in the tub, and although I have not lain in it since a child there is something familiar and comforting about it, even as the pepper continues to burn, on the outside of my body as well as the inside. Do I mind the smell? Not really, we are beyond the realm of embarrassment now, in another place entirely, a way of relating that is not 'her' and 'me' but the body as biological system, a place where the work of ingesting, digesting, defecating, and cell propagation gets done. Even when something gets smeared on my face it is okay. Why not? Am I not lying in a bathtub, will I not shortly be washed off in water that, though freezing (interesting contrast to the heat still inside), utterly cleanses me? I lie, exhausted, happy, indifferent observer of the occasional contractions in my colon.

"Stop joking." I say. "You're making makes me nervous."

"Have I joked with you, Chris? Has anything I told you would happen, not happened?"

"Not a joke, exactly. But a . . . thought experiment, as Einstein would say." Finding it easier, and more interesting, I have decided to assume her silence and reflexive questions as tact rather than idiocy.

"If a thought experiment is something we've both thought about, then I guess, yes, it is."

"Why should I want to die?" I asked. "I have a career, a great place to live, money, friends . . . everything."

"But you don't care about any of it. Nothing means anything to you, compared to what goes on in this room, where, for the first time in your life, someone understands you, knows exactly who you are, knows what the insides of you are like, knows what the smells of you are like, the liquids that pour out of your nose, your mouth, your eyes, your vagina, your urethra, your ass. . . ."

"You'd tell me if I were going to die, wouldn't you?"

A pause. "Yes." A longer pause. "Chris, you're going to die."

I hear this without flinching. My heart speeds up, as if in fear, but I feel no fear, only a sharpening of the senses and a huge sense of contentment. I am, after all, exhausted, an exhaustion not just of body but of mind and of soul....

"When?" I ask calmly.

"How should I know? I'm not god."

"*Oh.*" Relief, but also disappointment.

"You're not immortal. You're going to die. Surely you know this."

"I thought you meant, *with you.*"

"Is that really what you want?"

I begin to cry. Sadness, and a fatigue so deep, I have never, even in my deepest depressions, come near it. A fatigue so deep, I cannot imagine even picking up the phone to arrange for someone to clean my house, buy me food. How can I climb out of this tub, rinse myself off, get dressed, go home...?

She undoes my chains. I lie there, unmoving, as she dresses me.

70

"I want you to volunteer for something, Chris," she said the next time, even before I had gotten undressed.

"What is it, sir?" I asked.

"There are volunteers who know their assignments ahead of time, and those who do not. Which of these do you think deserves more respect?"

"The latter, sir."

"That is correct. Will you volunteer?"

"I don't know, sir. I'm scared."

"Have you been scared before?"

"Yes."

"Did you enjoy the feeling?"

"Yes ... I think so," I admit.

"Exactly! If humans lived in the moment, rather than in the past or the future, fear would be appreciated for the stimulus it lends to the entire body. Indeed, if it were not for the consequences, we would expose ourselves to the most dangerous environments, wouldn't we, rather than waste our money on cocaine and other drugs?"

"Yes sir."

"I am giving you the opportunity to repeat this sensation, and in a manner to which ahead of time you give your acquiescence, so you may fully savor the sentiment to its utmost."

"What are the possible consequences, sir?"

"No worse than that to which you alluded before. Of course, death is always a possibility, no matter what one does or doesn't do. I could order you to do this, and you would do it. But there are some missions that are so inherently risky, we commanders do not like to order our troops to undertake such; in such instances we prefer volunteers. Understand, I would not offer this opportunity to volunteer to all my subordinates. Only some even merit consideration as being worthy of such honors."

"Thank you, sir."

"So that you may not reproach me, even in your head, for not giving fair warning, let me say that the mission presents danger both to your body and your mind. It is probable you will emerge unscathed, but the risk is higher than that which one normally requires of one's subordinates. Indeed, it is conceivable it may violate one of the clauses of your enlistment."

"Which one, sir?"

"The one that says I may not cause you bodily harm."

I had known this, of course, but my heart lurched anyway. Of course I said "yes" – all the hormones, neurotransmitters, and receptors of my body urged me to do so, as did, oddly, my esthetic sense.

"That is good, soldier, very good, but no more than I expected. In anticipation of such I have invited some friends who you may be sure are very anxious to witness this event. I will signal them shortly."

"It's *now*?"

"Yes."

"But the contract promises me anonymity—" I protested.

"My friends will not know who you are, and if you do not so inform them they will never know. They will not address you, and you are not to address them. No one could recognize you – unless by chance some former lover is present, who may recognize certain special areas of your body. But surely you could trust them to keep silent! The others are only there because the spectacle will give them pleasure, and, in case something untoward happens, to be witnesses to your acquiescence to our endeavors."

"But—"

"The code word is of course still operative. But if I am forced to release you, they will of course learn who you are."

71

She led me into the bedroom and shackled me to the bed. Earphones were placed over my ears, through which techno music was played at a very high volume, so that I was unable to hear any other sound.

Sometime later, thirty minutes at least, but perhaps longer, for I had fallen asleep, the music was abruptly turned off and I was unshackled from the bed.

"Stand up," she ordered.

In the sudden silence all sounds seemed distorted.

"Are you nervous?" she asked.

"Yes. Will I be . . . raped?"

"How can there be rape where one has given consent?"

Utterly naked, save for my hood, I am led into the next room. Even the straps that bind my hands are off, to demonstrate that I am here of my own free will.

I am greeted with applause and whistles as well as a few coarse comments on my appearance.

"This is my slave, Chris. Chris is not her real name, but this is how she likes to refer to herself. Chris, will you display yourself for my friends and the camera."

I stand, rotating slowly in the poses she has taught me, bending over with my ass in the air, arching in the yoga bridge position, etc. She has shaved my pubic hair so that all parts of me are totally visible. All was silence, save for occasional whispers and what I felt, in my paranoia, was laughter. As I posed she touched various parts of my body with a cane, pointing out the darkness of my nipples, scars on my rear, dimples on my ass, etc. When the display was over she asked for their opinions on my appearance. These were many, and extended from the minute (a certain mole, an arthroscopic scar on my knee (had I been injured? yes; did the scars on my wrists indicate a suicide attempt? no)) to the general: that my legs were relatively short in relation to my torso, that I was older than they had expected but for my age relatively free of wrinkles, that a shaved pubic area on someone of my age was particularly obscene.

"What shape is she in?" someone asked.

"Her musculature is excellent, as she works out several times in a week in the gym. Shall I demonstrate?"

"Yes . . . of course . . . why not? . . . how amusing!" She told me to stick my rear in the air, then gave me a hard whack with the cane. "No dimpling, just a little redness," she pointed out. She pinched my skin, which hardly gave. "See how tight it is. Now watch this." She touched the cane to my asshole.

"That seems tight too," someone hooted.

"Not at all," she replied.

"Spread yourself," she ordered. Kneeling, with my head on the floor, I was able to relax sufficiently so that the cane could easily enter me. She told me to hold still, and pushed it in further, so that it seemed to tickle my insides almost to my bellybutton. Then she ordered me to roll forward onto my head so that the cane would stick straight up in the air. This was an awkward position, in which I was torn between worries of rolling over and snapping my neck, or having the cane pierce my insides. She told me to squeeze tight and, having satisfied herself by trying to push the cane in further to no avail, let go.

I managed, for a few seconds, by squeezing my sphincter muscles and shifting my weight, to hold the cane in the air. The room applauded.

"Very nice, Chris," someone said.

"Have you done such a thing before?"

"Please address any comments to my property to me," my owner reminded them.

"Since she's your property, how come she's not wearing ownership rings on her nipples or her lips?"

"We agreed to limit her external signs of servitude to a collar. Chris has been very insistent that this....*experience* not interfere with what she calls her 'real life.'" Laughter. "But tonight is real too, isn't it, Chris? Are you ready?"

"Yes sir."

"Are you in any way being forced to do anything against your will?"

"No, sir."

"Could you speak in complete sentences for the camera, Chris."

"Yes sir! Everything I do is totally voluntary," I said. "I allow what is to be done, to be done. In fact, I wish it."

"Very good." She snapped her fingers, and all of sudden what felt like hundreds of hands were on me, slathering me everywhere with what felt like Vaseline. I had heard of Canola oil parties, where everyone rolled around together on the slippery floor; could this be some gooier variant of that?

"Come here. This is a table. I would like you to lie down on it."

The table was high off the ground, like a pedestal.

I could hear the sighs of the wood on the floor as their bodies shuffled near, feel the warmth of their bodies and the exhalations as they breathed, the smell of meat and garlic and coffee and cigarettes emanating from their mouths and skin and hair. They stood there silently, surrounding me, breathing on me, animals in a pack.

"We will start in a minute. Chris, it will not be what you are imagining, it will seem strange and frightening, something that normally only happens to dead people, but this is not true, you will undergo something many other people have undergone, and quite safely. It does, however, have its dangers if you fight against it. But if you trust me, if you stay focused and calm, if you submit utterly to what is happening and concentrate only on the moment – and to live in the moment is what, in your 'real life,' you have so far been unable to do – everything will be fine. If you forget this it will be a difficult, unpleasant, and even dangerous experience. Are you ready?"

"Yes sir," I said. "I love you."

"See how even a sophisticated mind holds onto outmoded cliches," she pointed out.

"Bourgeois esthetics . . . ." someone snorted.

My left leg was lifted. I prepared myself for a crushing blow, or perhaps another demonstration with the cane, but instead some kind of fabric was wrapped around the instep and sole, then the toes, with the tightness of the fabric causing a slight loss of sensation. Then my right leg was raised and the same thing done. Then my hands and arms were bound, the fingers forced together as if I were wearing mittens.

Whereas normally one's arms might be bare with one's torso covered, here it was the reverse, so it was my torso which sensed the fabric on my limbs, and my arms and hands that felt nothing. There was no pain, only an overall pressure, and the feeling itself was not unpleasant.

As they worked they talked little, just simple directional comments such as "pull a little higher," or "now the left arm" or "don't forget the ears." With no pain at all being administered, or anything being poked into any of my orifices, their actions seemed businesslike and almost boring. I could not see what pleasure they could possibly derive from it, unless it was to cover me with the equivalent of a huge bandage. But why do this, unless one expected a huge amount of blood?

I struck outwards with my arms, but these were held to my sides as gauze was wrapped around my torso, binding my arms to it until I could no longer move. I kicked with my legs, but they too were grabbed and bound together, so I could do nothing but bang them up and down.

I tried to shout, but as I opened my mouth they clamped my jaws shut and wound the material around my head, both horizontally and vertically, leaving only a little opening through my mouth to breathe.

I was lifted up and placed on the floor. Due to the gauze covering my feet, I was unable to balance, and almost fell. Like a statue I wobbled back and forth until someone caught me. The only parts of me that could move were my nostrils and my throat, and these only with difficulty. I had to consciously clench my teeth and jaw to swallow, and I used the same effort to force open my nostrils to breathe as I did in the gym when raising the resistance on the Body Trek machine.

"Ready," someone said.

There was a slap, and a slight suction. Less a slap exactly, than a swabbing, as if I were being painted. Or lathered. An earthy smell, vaguely familiar, and a soothing coolness.

A straw was stuck up each nostril, in each ear, and in my mouth, poking a hole through the gauze, as they began to coat my face. I breathed out with great force, and one of the straws fell out. Someone immediately stuck it back in my nostril, pushing it as hard as it could go up the nose. With the exceptions of the little tunnels of air created by the straws, my entire head was soon covered, and they began to work on my body.

As the coating dried, it quickly grew warm. Sweat poured from my pores and mingled with the Vaseline in a kind of gooey soup that found its way into the tiniest crevices of my skin and toes. It reminded me of an Ayurvedic hot oil bath I had taken in India, and it kept the carapace from sticking to my skin. But the heat kept increasing, until I wondered whether the point was to cook me in my own juices.

I tried to cough the plaster dust out of my throat, but the thick saliva only clung to my vocal chords, further clogging my throat and making it even more difficult to breathe. I widened my nostrils to bring in air, but the width of the straws limited the amount I could suck in.

I began to panic. Surely I would die, from lack of water or air. Unable to communicate verbally, I tried shifting my weight so I would fall and my shell be broken. Even the revealing of my identity was better than this. But either because people were holding me up, or the plaster in which I was encased was itself the support, I remained upright.

I could think of nothing else to do. In the midst of all these people, I was no more able to make my feelings known than if I had been on a desert island.

I began to hyperventilate. In the past, pain had served to distract me from fear, but she had taken away pain's soothing discipline. My heart began to race, and I feared both passing out and a heart attack.

But at least if I passed out, I wouldn't know what was happening. Though no one would know if I were breathing or not.

Then the words she had spoken came to me: "if you trust me, if you remain focused and calm, if you submit utterly to what is happening and concentrate only on the moment –

everything will be fine." Alone in the dark and heat, having no other choice, I told myself to do as she said, to take it one breath at a time. I forced my diaphragm in and out, as if it were merely a muscle like any other, and told myself no harm could come to me, for I was a statue and what could happen to a piece of plaster?

"Is she dry now?" someone asked.

A faint knocking. "Yes."

The straws were pulled out of my nostrils and mouth, and it was slightly easier to breathe. If the heat itself did not actually lessen, it ceased to increase, so although I was as uncomfortable, at least I was no longer as frightened. I felt instead that it was I who was frightening, a Frankenstein, a golem, only whereas other monsters were inanimate objects brought to life, I was a living creature being made inanimate

They began to paint me: bright pink for my skin, black to "outline" breasts and hips and facial features, blue for the eyes, "streetwalker red" for my lips, or at least so they said. It was odd, being both invisible yet the center of attention.

Things began spinning. I was lifted, tilted, spun. Presumably I was being carried someplace, but carelessly, with no attention to the direction of my head, or whether I got nauseous. Fear made me lose control of my bodily functions; I could smell and feel stuff moving down my leg.

When they stopped I was placed face up on a slab, a tablecloth spread over me. Knives and forks were placed on me, bottles of expensive wines and liqueurs. Toast were made: to *The Village Voice*, to Personals, to private post boxes and the institution of slavery-hood as it was currently instituted in the western world. One person, evidently Negroid, remarked on the psychological value of employing whites thusly as a way to redress former inequities. The growing popularity of such relationships in this age of sexual boredom and degeneracy was applauded, and a fervent prayer uttered that it would continue to flourish and grow. So my master was black, and I a token in the redressing of historical wrongs. How could I object?

A selection of Beluga and Sevruga caviars was offered, and goose liver pate, and several cheeses whose malodorous fumes nonetheless made my stomach churn with hunger. After further speeches the main courses were brought forth: quenelles and duck confit and steak from hand-massaged cattle from Japan.

The historical role of sexual subjugation was discussed, how it waxed and waned in various periods, how war and income inequalities nourished it, how financial prosperity reduced it, and how now, with the judicious employment of the Internet, ways might be found to increase the traffic of persons across international borders. The question of volition was broached, and a schism revealed, between those who insisted on the wholly voluntary character of slavehood and those who, referring to de Sade, spoke of the right to kidnap, torture, and murder. Reference was made to the current slave trade in Africa, not so much to emulate it, but with a suggestion that one could study its modes of recruitment, distribution, and public relations, with particular emphasis on the way it managed to frustrate not just action but even consultation concerning it by the press and other nation states.

Extreme measures were discussed, ways to dispose of property rendered useless by physical impairments both accidental and intentional, or of those who, once repudiated, refused to accept their dismissal and threatened to go the press or the police ("slavery is not, after all, a substitute for the welfare system"): such as, drugging them and then burying them alive or throwing them in the river with metal weights attached to their feet, or pushing them out the window of a private airplane, or (when such methods are too flamboyant), dismembering them and grinding them in sink garbage disposal systems (not available in New York, alas!), or by entombment in statues and such like. References were made to specific works of art (several of which I knew) in which bits of skin, ground bone, etc. from former slaves could be traced, were the police savvy enough to check.

"What about Chris?" someone asked.

"She knows too much."

"Has the question of termination ever been broached?"

"Shh ... what if she can hear?"

"Don't worry. We stuffed her ears. She can hear nothing save her own heartbeat."

I tried to shout, but over the talk and clatter of dishes and music I could not be heard.

Burning, slicing, carving into little pieces to be roasted, or broiled, or barbecued, even consumed raw ... they mentioned it all. Although I kept telling myself it was just a joke, that my owner had a more elaborate sense of humor and imagination than I had hitherto given her credit for, I was nonetheless petri-fied – if only by the contents of their imagination, far more depraved and debauched than I would have thought possible. And yet are not the sensations of fear – increased pulse, shallow breathing, warmth of body – indistinguishable from those of arousal? Later, when they are bored, when the question of my disposal is abandoned, I am hoisted into the air, suspended horizontally by chains from which I swing freely. Like a swing or cradle I am pushed, back and forth, back and forth, on occasion banging the wall; I can hear bits of the dried plaster fall in chunks on the floor. Then I am hung upside down by my ankles, like a carcass in a butcher shop. Often, without success, I had tried to do a headstand; it is oddly satisfying to do so now. I feel clear-headed, as if I were doing yoga. Above my head my feet swing back and forth, back and forth, as if my head were a pendulum of a clock. No, I am like a rocket ship, a planet, a star in the center of this little world; not even a star, but a glitch in the space-fabric that manifests as matter, a conglomeration of probability vectors and loci of energy and random fluctuations in the vacuum of space....

Am I really hanging upside down, like a carcass of beef? Or is this just the escape fantasy of a person who in fact spends her days encased in a straitjacket in a hospital for the insane somewhere in upper New York State?

What is my name?

What do I do?

Where do I live?

My position was returned to the upright, and it was "discovered" that indeed, my ears had not been covered.

"Oh dear! Then perhaps...."

"Not the first time."

"But this is very bad!"

"She's too far gone to care," my owner assured them.

"In any case, no help for it now."

"Shit happens."

My ears were finally plastered, so I heard no more. Save what sounded like a drumbeat (though perhaps it could have been the rumbling of cars by the building, or even the beating of my heart), and a high-pitched hum – perhaps also music – but maybe the circulation of my blood, or fear.

72

Later, much later, when the plaster has been removed, when my body is cleaned up, when I have been permitted to sleep, when I have remembered who I am, when I have emerged, uncertain of date or time, into the street, hunger overwhelms me. To my shock, the restaurant is open. Either I have lost an entire day, or much less time has passed than I thought. As if in a dream, I walk towards it. As if in a dream, I pick up the menu. The dream is my own, I have been here before, in what is called 'the real world.' But it is when the real world is at its realest that it seems most like a dream, or a movie. The lights are on my face, is it a movie? Yes, the one I have been starring in my whole life. I shift on the enameled metal seat, and because I am so thoroughly in my body I feel through my shorts (or think I feel) my skin slightly falling through the little holes in the seat where the pattern (kind of an abstract round flower) has been stamped. I don't have to look at it to know what it looks like, though I am not conscious of ever having consciously thought about it. Wouldn't it be ironic if later, at home, these little creases in the shape of flowers were the sole objective correlatives of this night?

I order my Standard Meal: fish, plantains, flan. I am conscious, again, of my swallowing.

The breadbasket is empty. I must have eaten everything.

I think about what I was thinking about that I could not

remember whether the breadbasket was on the table or not when I sat down. I cannot remember.

The silverware is slimy and cold. My sweat or the waiter's sweat or grease from the dishwater? I wipe the fork off with my napkin, embarrassed to let the waiter see me, as if I must conceal from him my knowledge of the restaurant's faulty hygiene practices, as if to excuse myself for not running away in disgust.

We who are about to die do not care about microbes.

But in fact, I cannot eat. I raise and lower the fork, which is so clammy, to my lips, which has a moustache of sweat which drips salt in my mouth. The piece of fish with the fried skin travels up and down through the air, its eye so close to my eye that it begins to hypnotize me. Does it care that it is dead? Does it remember the net, or being scooped out of the water, or the feel of a cleaver down its middle? or is its last memory that of other fish pressing tighter and tighter as the water drains out and the net rises skyward in sickening motion....?

73

Before taking a cab I stop at the deli. I buy what I have never bought before. They sit there, in my kitchen, little cans of baby food. Peas and carrots, chicken, peaches, remarkably like the Cuisinart pureed veggies nouvelle cuisine restaurants began to serve years ago, but far, far cheaper.

I am not frightened when I eat this food.

74

Home, I turn on the tv. This is what's real, these little dots of color flickering many times a second, and the noise these little dots make. I am a toy. I do not exist. I am nothing.

This is not depressing, but relaxing.

Ever since I can remember I have thought about the best time to die. Whether it is better when one is happy, knowing life can only go downhill, or when one is so unhappy that the presumed alleviation of misery exceeds the terrible poignancy of death.

I still don't know.

5.
Freedom

75

One day, after I had arrived and undressed as was my custom, she said: "Our relationship has become tedious to me. I'm tired of your complaints, your groveling, your protestations of love. It's all so predictable: my commands, your disobediences, the punishments. No doubt you feel this way yourself?"

"Not at all," I said, astonished. "I've never been less bored in my life."

"I believe you, but frankly, I'm surprised – you seem to consider yourself a person of such discrimination. Perhaps it is merely that what transpires between us is more unique for you than it is for me. But whether it comes from varying experience or a lower tolerance of boredom, surely you can understand my ennui?" I didn't, but of course I nodded my assent. "Good. For I'd like you to assent to a slight change in our contract. It's a small one, but of course you must agree...." She paused, and I wondered what it could be – extending its length? breaking up with the Current? a branding of my torso? "It involves wearing a device that prevents you from speaking."

"A gag, you mean?" I asked, feeling some disappointment at the triviality of the request.

"Not exactly, though the effect will be the same. But even when you're not wearing such a device – such as when I telephone you with an order – you're still not to talk to me."

"But what if I need to tell you something? Or I don't understand some command?"

"Infants and animals can't talk, but they manage to convey their needs very well. One consequence, of course, is that you'll no longer be able to use the code words. But you might as well know, physical pain will no longer be a major component of our relationship. It takes too long, and I have to work too hard, to begin to approach the threshold of pain at which further punishment becomes efficacious. It's as if you decided to demonstrate that, of all human beings in the world, you're the one most willing to undergo any sort of agony or torment – as if such perversity and stubbornness were something to be proud rather than ashamed of! No! No longer will I cater to your vanity by using your body like a pincushion, or a carcass to be carved, or a sewer into which the world pours its bodily effluvia. I am, however, willing to assign a new role and tasks to you."

Naturally I was confused and upset, less by the elimination of the code words than being unable to communicate my thoughts and feelings. What, after all, could be more distressing for a writer? And it was the memory of the words I said to her, as much as any act, that filled my fantasies when I was not with her. But although I continued to protest, she was adamant: either I acquiesced without further discussion to what was required, or our contract would be terminated and I banished from her presence forever. Since I found latter impossible, I agreed. Thus, after final protestations of love, and begging that she would make up for my lack of speech by an augmentation of hers, our new life together began.

76

I was to live it on my hands and knees, with a leash around my neck attached to a collar. My arms were linked by a chain, as were my legs, so that I could separate them only by the width of my body. Different chains connected my right wrist and right ankle, and my left wrist and left ankle, so that even should I try I would not be able to stand on two legs. A strap was placed under my tongue that prevented me from speaking in comprehensible fashion, although I would be able to mouth the barks, woofs, yips, and yelps of doggy vocalizations.

She taught me the various canine commands – "sit," "heel," "stay" and so forth – first in response to her voice, then by movements of the leash, and how to shake hands or rise up, panting, on my hind legs. She bounced endless balls to me; by listening carefully, I learned to figure out where they had gone and how to retrieve them. I was forced to lie for hours sniffing old shoes and sweaty tee-shirts, so that I might become familiar with her smell. She taught Charlie and me how to walk together, side-by-side, without nipping or jostling.

As promised, she inflicted few corporal punishments. Even when she did, these were generally so mild in nature it was more like the iconography of pain than pain itself. This was so frustrating that I found the content of my fantasies changing. Whereas I used to dream of unspeakable sexual acts, I was now haunted by images of overwhelming physical punishments.

These made me wet in exactly the same way.

Over time, she modified my appearance. My fingers were bound together so I could not use my hands in the normal fashion; pads were placed under my palms and over my knees. A tail was added, which she hung from a chain she placed around my waist. I was unable to manipulate it, but grew to like its weight hanging off me, the tickle of its fur against my ass. She replaced the leather in my mouth with a metal chain that went under my tongue and attached to my collar. Its sharp angles cut my tongue; the only method of relieving the pain was to let my jaw hang open. Saliva spooled at the end of my tongue until it reached the critical mass to drool; the dryness of my throat made me pant.

One thing I had great difficulty with was in learning to bark like a dog. Although I made myself hoarse imitating Charlie, my cries remained hopelessly human. "It's your vanity," she accused. "You insist on remaining apart from the pack, as if you're some-how better than the others." She consigned me to a corner for the rest of the day as she played with Charlie, and left me alone as they took a walk.

For a long time I rested on my paws, awaiting their return. But as time passed a feeling of terrible loneliness came over me. I used my new sniffing powers to find her closet and, overcome by a desire I could not explain, I laid down on top of her shoes. One smelled particularly pungent, and I began to chew on it, less from hunger (although I had not eaten in some time) than to comfort myself. I soon fell asleep.

When she came back she berated me for ruining her shoe. Holding it in front of my nose, she beat me on the rear with a rolled-up newspaper. This was a sad contrast to the beatings of the past, but I pretended it hurt and yelped as loudly as I could.

Later, however, she confessed her pleasure: not only that I had expressed my anger in such a canine fashion, but that in her absence I had not tried to undo my chains or pull the hood off my head.

I deserved neither the praise nor the treat, for the thought of freeing myself had not even occurred to me.

Until this point I'd been naked, or nearly so, but one day, when I was standing quietly in the pointer position, she presented me with my "coat," which she said was made from the skin of a dead dog. There was no way for me to know if this was true, but its texture and smell were certainly mammalian in nature.

This costume came in two parts. The bottom slipped on like a pair of tights, but with a huge cutout area leaving bare my crotch and anus. The top was pulled over my head, like a sweater cut high and short, so that it covered my arms but stopped above the nipples. The skin felt soft and supple against my body, the fur longer and finer than Charlie's.

At first Charlie seemed confused by my costume, sniffing me repeatedly as if he did not know who I was. But he quickly grew accustomed to it, seeming to prefer it to my natural skin and treating me more as a fellow canine. We chased each other around furniture and sang bizarre contrapuntal canine duets. But my barks still didn't please her, and other things as well. She took to placing me in a cage for extended periods of time. Sometimes I didn't even know what I'd done wrong, but was punished anyway. Was it possible that, even in this new role, she was becoming tired of me?

The cage was so small it was difficult to change position, let alone rise up on my legs. Mostly I lay on my paws, or fell asleep for an indeterminate period of time. Increasingly I was unable to gauge the amount of time I'd spent with her. More than once I emerged from her building to find myself in the light of a new day, or even the twilight of the next. This confusion about time caused me to miss the few remaining appointments I'd been allowed to make, and because I could offer no coherent explanation of my behavior to friends or acquaintances, I ceased entirely making any plans.

77

One day, after some instruction in dog show technique, she put
some dried food in a bowl for Charlie. He grunted and snorted
as he ate; bits of food flew out of his mouth onto me. Usually
she fed me right after him – human food, like tuna or liverwurst,
although in a bowl on the floor – but this time she did not. Having
been ordered to abstain from food the previous 24 hours, I
began to whimper.

"Okay," she said, as if placating a child, "I'll give you a treat."
This generally meant only a cookie or cracker, but it was better
than nothing, and I obediently rose up on my hind legs. But as
I bit into it, I realized from its hard texture and meaty smell it
was not my usual cracker but a "dog bone." At first I resisted,
but she stroked my nose and behind my ears in a manner so
comforting, especially in contrast to her recent belittling of me,
that I did as she desired. Although the idea was revolting, the
taste was not that terrible.

Charlie snorted and thumped his tail, perhaps in jealousy,
and I felt his warmth breath on my face. I turned my head away,
but she ordered me to remain still as he licked my nose and
eyelids. Even when he stopped, his mouth must have remained
open, for a few drops of saliva landed on my lips. I began to
retch.

"Lick him back," she said.

I waited, then, with great reluctance, extended my tongue.
Evidently it was a part of the body in which Charlie had only
minimal interest, for he barely touched it with his own. I was torn
between immediately pulling my tongue back into my mouth, so
he could not lick it further, or keeping it extended, so his saliva

would evaporate from it before I put it back in my mouth.

I heard the sound of a can being punctured, the round blade of the can opener rotating. The clunk of a spoon as it knocked against the side of a bowl, footsteps as she walked over to me and placed the bowl on the floor in front of my face and ordered me to eat it.

Whereas the cracker was dry and relatively odorless, the smell of the wet meat was strong and pungent. I have always been inordinately afraid of vomiting. Breathing only through my mouth so I would not smell it, I touched my lips to the cold wet meat. Can I really do this? I thought. In the moral sense it did not compare to spreading my legs for Charlie, but on the visceral level it was somehow more disgusting. Charlie had only had dry food, and tried to push me aside so he could have the food himself. I happily made way for him, but my owner pulled him away and pushed my head into the bowl. Some of the food entered my mouth and some slid up my nostrils, making it difficult to breathe. "Swallow," she commanded. At first I wouldn't, but she held my nose in the meat until I was completely unable to breathe.

Tears in my eyes, stomach retching, I acquiesced. After several more mouthfuls Charlie was allowed to join me. I felt the cold wet of his nose, the tickle of his whiskers, as side by side we ate the food – he devouring, I as slowly as was permitted. Afterwards he licked me, slobbering bits of wet meat on my face, then I could hear him lapping up water. I put my own face in the water, in hopes of washing off the food and saliva. But some meat stuck in my nostrils, like little dried up balls of snot.

In the other acts of degradation, there had always been the mitigating factor of physical sensation, but now there was only humiliation. In my rage and anger I began to howl. It sounded so much like a dog's, at first I did not realize where it was coming from. "At last!" she exclaimed. "You sound like a real canine." Charlie joined in, and indeed, for once my cries were indistinguishable from his.

78

The next time I was in her presence, she told me of a further change in our arrangements. Up until then I had a special bark to let her know when I needed to go to the bathroom, but had continued to use a regular toilet. But it was absurd, was it not, for a dog to sit on a toilet as if it were a human? In the future I was to go on all fours, as canines did.

I barked vociferously – this was worse even than the dog food! Ignoring my complaints, she brought me to my cage, where she left me with a bowl of water, telling me she should be back for me in due time.

It was a very hot day, but although I dipped my face in the bowl to cool myself, I refused to drink, knowing this would only hasten the moment when I would have to use the bathroom.

Eventually she came to get me. She led me to a kind of litter box and ordered me to get in it on all fours. It felt familiar, not that unlike sandboxes I'd played in as a child, perhaps even peed in by mistake. I told myself it was not so terrible, that it was something Esmeralda did several times a day, regardless of who was in the room with her, and why should it be any different for me?

Nonetheless, I stood immobile, tears pouring out of my eyes

in shame. "Here or in your cage, it's all the same to me," she said, and hooked the leash on me to bring me back to the cage. Only then did I go, so I should not have to lie in my own sticky juices.

"I knew it, you're such a good dog," she said, in a taunting manner. When she bent down to pet me I opened my mouth and sunk my teeth into her wrist.

The move was instinctive, less a bite than a grab, as if to remind her of my power. But when she tried to resist, I sunk my teeth in deeper. The skin tore and I enjoyed for the first time the heady salty taste of blood. I felt an intense desire to crunch my teeth through her bones, one that had as much to do with a kind of primeval impulse toward the consumption of raw flash as with anger. But I was also frightened of her, and filled with a kind of love, so I did nothing, and she pulled away her arm.

Her fury was indescribable: she lashed my collar to a post so I could not move, placed a muzzle over my jaws, then lashed me with a bullwhip until, when I was on the verge of passing out, she switched to a paddle. I awoke up to alcohol being rubbed into my wounds. Then I passed out again from the pain. When I was alert enough again, she resumed her beating.

I have no recollection of when it stopped, but even when it did, and for a long time after, the sound of my howls, then whimpers, filled the room. "At least you sound like a dog now." she said.

It was very late when I left; almost no one was on the street. Throughout the beating, I'd managed to avoid a second visit to the litter box. But out on the street I could control myself no longer, and I found myself squatting between two cars and relieving myself, to further tears of humiliation and shame.

79

The next day I woke in a rage. I decided that no matter what happened, I would never see her again. What could she do – tell the Current? I didn't even care if she knew who I was and exposed me to the world. Such kind of publicity, in this peculiar age, might even help my career. I left the special phone at home and went to the health club for the first time in weeks. The water was soothing; each stroke helped to wipe away my shame. As I dressed I listened in wonder to the women in the locker room, chattering innocently about their jobs or the guys they were dating. How lucky they were! How pathetic!

I went to a restaurant to celebrate my liberation, but a sense of anxiety began to build in me. It was not enough to say good-bye: I needed to tell her exactly how I felt.

So I returned to my apartment and the phone, rehearsing all the while what I would say, both in my head and out loud.

But the phone did not ring. Long before, she had made me throw away my tranquilizers, my painkillers, my anti-depressants, my alcohol, my drugs, so I paced about the apartment in a rage I could not control. Night came, and I could not sleep. By the next day I had developed a massive headache which made it impossible to eat.

In frustration, I opened the doors to my kitchen cabinets, grabbed some dishes, and began throwing them against the walls and floor. The action and noise was soothing, but soon the pieces became too small to break. So I found a hammer and began to bang, not caring a bit about my beautiful maple floors. I half-hoped someone in my building would hear me and call the police: jail, perhaps, would be a distraction. But I lived in a renovated factory building, with ceilings and floors made of concrete. Either no one heard me, or – more likely – no one cared.

I was lying in the porcelain dust when the phone finally rang. She told me that she had called once, and when I hadn't answered, decided that, rather than punish me in the usual fashion, she would show me how miserable I was be without her, how utterly dependent on her and her commands. I was so relieved to hear her voice I started to cry, and all thoughts of speeches went out of my head. I barked what I hoped sounded like an apology and immediately made my way to her. From then on I ceased even token resistance to her requests, no matter how disgusting or bizarre, so that when in fact I was finally ordered to have intercourse with Charlie, the pleasure I allowed myself, paradoxically, was no longer merely conceptual, as it had been in that long-ago time (scarcely two months previously) when I had initially agreed to the contract, but physical, for I had learned to appreciate that Charlie and I were both sentient beings who, from other sides of the species and language divide, were able to partake of shared sensations and emotions.

When I hinted at such to Leslie, her stomach turned in disgust, but was it really so different from being turned on by a human being of another nationality and language, such as occurred between John Smith and Pocahontas, or the *Bounty* mutineers when they landed on Tahiti? I think not.

Charlie's penis was not large, of course, compared to a human's, and, by ejaculating almost instantaneously, he made no attempt to consciously prolong my pleasure; on the other hand, I being ordered to hold him to me as long as possible, his struggle to disentangle himself caused me great satisfaction, however unintentional on his part. My hair and body soaked with perspiration, my owner kindly cradled my head in her arms as Charlie pushed against me, complimenting me upon the degrees to which I would go to prove myself worthy of her attentions, and the empathy and "fraternity" (in the French sense of the word) with which I was able to commune with a member of another species.

"You are a true canine," she said, as she petted me, and I was grateful for the remark, as I was grateful for the canned food with which she rewarded our acrobatics, and of which, after all (according to the newspapers) a portion of our elderly routinely partake.

On the way home I usually purchased a Häagen Daz ice cream bar, partly because the dog food (albeit nutritious) stimu- lated my craving for sugar, and partly to erase the meaty flavor from my mouth.

I stared at myself in the mirror after one such occasion. It had been scarcely past midnight when I had left her building, the streets full of revelers, with whom I felt an incredible camaraderie, as if, not subject to her proscriptions, I could go home with any or all and happily perform whatever acts came into our heads. Indeed, as I walked past female couples in the East Village, I began to wonder how it would be to command them to perform such acts together with an animal I should myself acquire, more out of novelistic curiosity than sexual desire – to experience life, as it were, from the other side of the mirror. How many others, I wondered, harbored similar such ambitions in their hearts? I felt extraordinarily light and bright, as if I'd taken just the right amount of cocaine and could stay up, with the same degree of alertness, for days.

My face in the mirror reflected my happiness. My degradation had brought me through the dark tunnel and out the other side, so that, contrary to habit, I lay in bed without washing or brushing my teeth, my arms spread wide, as if to welcome whatever phantoms would come in the night.

80

On the next visit my costume was again altered, so that my ass, genitals, and nipples as well as the rest of me were covered in animal skin. I began to sweat, and the heat and moistness brought out the odors of the skin, making me nauseous. "Hot, isn't it?" my owner asked. I yelped my assent, and drank contentedly out of the water bowl that I had so recently scorned. "Nice night for a walk, don't you think?" I yelped again. "I think I'll take Charlie to the park. Come on, Charlie!" she shouted.

I felt my usual abandonment when they left, but almost immediately I heard them come back up the stairs. In happiness I ran over and licked her. She scratched behind my ears. "You've been such a good dog I think you deserve a treat. How would you like to take a walk with me and Charlie? You're well enough trained, aren't you, not to embarrass your owner in public? Charlie, should we take her?" And I heard her pick up my leash.

I barked furiously. Neither the original nor revised contract had anything in it about exposing me to people. Although I had performed for her friends in private, this seemed different. I ran to my favorite refuge, a closet off the kitchen from which she always had difficulty extracting me.

"I know what you're thinking," she said. "But the agreement was not that you would not *appear* in public, but that your *anonymity* would be preserved. Dressed as you will be, no one could possibly recognize you, and there will be additional pads under your palms and on your knees to protect them from glass, etc.

"You will be on a leash, of course, and will walk by my side and Charlie's, obeying all my commands. You will hold yourself erect, your back straight, your head raised and alert. People may try to pet you; if so, let them. Do not bite. If other dogs approach, let them sniff and play with you – unless, of course, I command you not to.

"At a certain point you may find a need to relieve yourself. You will tug three times on your leash to inform me of this, at which time I will place a newspaper under you and you will do your business, squatting on all fours, as you do in the apartment."

She took my head in her hands and caressed me gently. "Believe me, the fact that I trust you to do this is a great honor, and marks how far you and I have both come. Public display is not something that could have been done in the beginning of our relationship; indeed, I have never reached such a stage with a dog so quickly, especially one with so little prior training. I wonder, sometimes, if there had been no time limit... In any case," she sighed, "as you have put your trust in me, I put mine in you. It is not inconceivable that some figure of authority may approach to question us. If such occurs, I will reply that we are rehearsing a scene for a movie in which humans play the part of dogs. Even if, under the direst of circumstances, I am forced to remove the metal from your mouth and you are commanded to speak, you shall agree with everything I say.

"If in this or any other matter you disobey me, your costume will immediately be removed, and you will be on the street naked, a stray, with no keys, no clothing, no money, no identification. Eventually the police will find you, but you will not be able to pretend that what happened to you was involuntary – not with the photos and videos." And she catalogued in concise but pungent detail the contents of several of the videotapes in her possession.

She fed me a plate of what seemed rather coarse pate, from a special bowl which Charlie was forbidden to share. It had a slightly medicinal cherry taste, not unpleasant in itself, though it contrasted somewhat oddly with the pate.

"You have just swallowed a laxative," she informed me when I was done. "It should take effect within an hour or so. It will ensure your having to relieve yourself by the time we reach the park, and you can show everyone how well you've learned your lessons."

'Show everyone?' I had thought there was no further level I could sink to, but now I discovered I was wrong.

Before we left she had me sit on my haunches, and placed what felt like a heavy helmet over my head. It was warm and hard to breathe through, with a sickly smell of animal and formaldehyde. It weighed so much I had trouble holding my neck parallel to the ground, as one does when walking on all fours, and its nose must have been long and pointy, for I subsequently found myself banging it, more than once, into a wall. "How handsome you look," she said. "All the other dog owners will be jealous of me." And the three of us headed out of the apartment.

81

I started downstairs head-first, in the usual fashion, but when I lifted my front paws to lower myself I slid forward almost into a somersault. Only by rolling into the bannister and pressing myself against it could I get myself to stop. After this I went down sideways, lowering one leg over the edge horizontally and then bringing the other down to meet it, like sidestepping down a ski slope. It was slow and cumbersome, and my crotch became stretched from the angle of the steps. The warm air against the cold marble made the steps very slippery, and the stone cut into my knees.

The downstairs door opened and I heard people entering the building. Their feet made a peculiar echo I didn't recall hearing before, perhaps due to my proximity to the stone through which the sound was carried – a much better medium of transmission than air. They must have entered an apartment on a floor below, for the sounds of their walking and talking abruptly ceased.

Then a door next to us opened, and I heard steps, and smelled garbage.

"Another movie?" a man's voice asked, with a hint of irony.

"Yes," said my master. "What do you think of my new 'leading lady'?"

"'Led' lady, you mean," he said. "Very fine. A mastiff, I think, with perhaps a bit of shepherd mixed in."

"Husky too, and she's got a bit of the wolfhound in her as well." She ordered me to shake the man's hand, and I carefully extended a paw.

"Good dog," he said, petting me in approbation.

"You don't happen to have any old bones for her?" my master inquired.

"Perhaps I do. Let me see." The garbage bag was opened and I was forced to paw through it for a bone, which I located amidst the rotting salad, soggy napkins, and sharp tops of tuna cans. I was ordered to eat it, but what little meat there was smelled rotten, and a piece of aluminum foil reacted unpleasantly with the silver of my fillings. I began to feel grateful for the laxative.

Gradually they lost interest in me and began discussing someone called "Chip." My owner knew Chip, but did not like him. Other names were mentioned too, some of which clearly belonged to people, others perhaps to dogs, but whether a dog like me or a dog like Charlie, I couldn't tell. After awhile, no doubt tiring of our slow pace, the neighbor left us. I heard his quick steps down the stairs, and mourned the ease of human locomotion.

Finally we reached the street. The air was refreshing, even with the smell of automobile exhaust and a kind of sick perfume-y smell from a tree whose name I am always unable to remember. Honeysuckle? Hyacinth?

The brown stone of the exterior steps was soft and warm, less slippery than the stone of the stairs. It was wonderful to finally be on flat ground, to no longer have to worry about slipping and breaking my neck. The warmth of the stone also helped calm my stomach, which was churning unpleasantly from the bone, the laxative, and the exertion.

My owner let me rest a bit, then jerked me upright to descend the final steps to the pavement. Bits of raised stone embedded in it dug through the pads on my limbs, almost as if a pattern were being engraved on my skin. I had played hopscotch and other such games on similar sidewalks in my childhood, and often returned upstairs with crisscross patterns embossed on my palms and knees.

"Heel," she commanded. I was trying to keep up with her and Charlie, but due to fatigue and stomach distress, I could barely move. I bumped into something. Metal. Smooth. Then a softer substance that smelled like tar, but also, oddly, arugula. A tire. It felt warm and slightly sticky, and beyond the arugula odor I could detect that of the rubber it was made from.

A second tire (a hint of excrement this time), then I was ordered from the pavement into the street. I tried to resist but the leash cut into my collar and I was forced to crawl into the gutter.

The tar on the street was softer still against my knees, and I began to enjoy its smoothness and warmth. Eventually, having recognized that I had become "dirty," that I had been irrevocably tainted by the street, that I was in no sense the person I had been, I began to sniff the tires of other cars almost with curiosity, not resisting even when she ordered me to smell some disgusting mess placed there by some canine. I worried, of course, about contamination by dogshit, but then recalled that in some sense I *was* a dog, and if I wasn't a dog I was another kind of animal – an animal whose bite was more dangerous than a dog's and whose shit perhaps was too. So maybe it was I who was the menace to civilization, and not the other way around.

I had been blocking out my need to go to the bathroom, but fire soon poured through my insides, and I found it necessary to tug three times on my leash. She adjusted my costume, and suddenly I felt the moist and cool night air upon my rear, and a newspaper placed under me, I did my business. Feces began to exit my body in hot, noisy spurts, with a strong but not totally repugnant meat-like smell. A vision of myself in Morocco, feverish and ill, squatting all night over a hole in the floor, filled my mind. There had been newspapers there also, instead of toilet paper, and I had been alone, ill and far from home. Surely that was worse. I tried to prevent my befoulments from soiling my costume, but cramps would wash over me and I would forget everything save emptying myself. Feeling feverish, I lay with my head against her knee, for by now she was squatting next to me, scratching behind my ears and telling me what a good dog I was and how proud, how very proud, she was of me.

I could hear people passing by. It hardly seemed possible they could notice nothing unusual, but I heard no comments pertaining to me or my situation.

After this, heading to the park seemed less punishment than treat. Indeed, the soft dirt of the dog run was comforting. Strange canines ran up to sniff and mount me, but my owner managed to pull me away before any such encounters could be consummated. It was a pleasure to roll on the grass, now that the gutter had burned the fear of dirt and feces out of me. Even when other dog owners or the homeless or alkies made disparaging references to my appearance, I felt protected, for my master made it clear she was proud of my demeanor and deportment. Would every canine could say as much!

Upstairs, after a climb that was easier than the one down, she held my hand as I squatted in the tub and expelled the remaining foods and liquids from my system. Then she bathed me in warm soapy water, all the while telling me what a good dog I was, how well I had undertaken my training, how pleased she was that we had reached this new level. Several times the tub was emptied and refilled till any remaining smell of shit and garbage was gone. Then she tenderly patted me dry and rubbed lotion over me and put salve on my scrapes and wounds. Too exhausted from the various insults to mind and body to attempt to move, I lay there, almost in an out-of-body state, as with a toothbrush and toothpaste she brushed my teeth for me, and had me rinse my mouth out with mouthwash. Then she brought a blanket that she wrapped around me. I slept that night in the tub next to Charlie, our bodies curled around each other for comfort and warmth.

82

From then on I abandoned all pretense at normal existence. I ceased paying bills, and returned phone calls only when I knew I'd reach an answering machine. Soon I didn't even bother doing that. People still left the occasional message, but these concerned events that seemed increasingly remote, and I deleted them without listening. After telling the Current I was going through some "stuff" and would speak to her when I felt better, and Leslie that I was going out of town with a married woman I was having an affair with, I disconnected the machine and answered only the phone with the unlisted number.

I did little save lie on the bed and wait for her calls. Reading became impossible, groups of incomprehensible words about trivial events and people it was inconceivable anyone could be interested in. Even tv narrative bored me. I flipped through the channels like a deck of cards, not for the content but the visuals. Sometimes I'd turn on the stereo, and find it was already on, or

I'd play two or three radio stations on my different machines at the same time. My behavior didn't alarm me; I decided it was my duty to immerse myself in this experience as deeply as possible so that when it was over I could use it in my writing. To this end, and also because I had become used to it, I began eating my food and drinking my water out of bowls I placed on the floor and shared with Esmeralda. It was, oddly, a very peaceful life.

83

Although on occasion my master had casually mentioned a "dog show," I had assumed it was an indefinite and probably fictitious event rather than something specific I might actually be taken to. I was therefore both surprised and alarmed when, one afternoon, after donning my costume, she informed me that we would be going to a place where I should find myself in the presence of other dogs and their owners.

"Be sure to be on your best behavior, or no one will want you," she warned.

Want me? What could she mean?

I was ordered into my cage. She said that although she personally trusted me to be on good behavior, the rules of "the Society" compelled her to place a muzzle on me. Her footsteps moved away, and I was alone. Nervous about this "Society," and uncertain what she meant by the idea of "nobody wanting me," the powerlessness of my position overwhelmed me. But she paid no attention to my sobbing, and eventually I fell asleep.

I woke to the sound of people talking.

"...twice tried to bite me," my owner was saying.

"Kara's dog managed to escape, but we caught her on Tenth Street," someone said.

"...hard for them to get far...."

"Are we ready?"

"I think so."

"Heave-ho."

My cage was lifted and carried. They didn't do it very carefully, and my body rolled from side to side. There were abrupt starts and stops, each of which occasioned further bruises; then I was evidently being transported down the stairs, for gravity pushed me helplessly towards the bottom of the cage, my body at such an angle that I had to push with all my might to prevent my neck from being crushed.

Finally we reached the street: car exhaust and garbage smells and the occasional whiff of dog excrement and piss.

A door slammed, then another, as the cage was put down. Then I heard, as if from a great distance, a motor starting.

"God, it's like a kennel in here."

"Are you going to let her out?" someone asked.

"She's been misbehaving all day."

"She's being auctioned off?"

"Of course. It was part of the original plan."

"Difficult, though, isn't it?"

"There's no room for sentimentality in our work," someone sighed.

"One has one's life to live, after all."

A dog named "Pepper" was introduced to "Brownie," and ordered to shake hands. Laughter, then I heard the moans of someone who sounded more human than dog, perhaps the canine whose name was "Pepper," as she was forced to play (who knows in what fashion) with "Brownie." Then the van stopped, and yet another 'dog' and its owner were deposited into our midst. As our group grew, the discussion became increasingly lively and raucous, with many mysterious and alarming references to where we were going and what was to follow.

After what seemed like hours, we reached our destination. My cage was removed from the van, and I put on my leash. The ground was rough and hard, and the air smelled of fish and gasoline, and perhaps a whiff of salt. Were we near the water? Around me I could hear the clanking of leashes, and the soft growls and barks as other dogs and I were jostled together into what seemed a slowly moving line.

84

Until now I had remained relatively calm. But panic began to churn my insides, as I heard a woman quite near us being asked questions concerning the provenance of her German shepherd in some detail before being told to proceed to the "auction area."

"And what breed is *this*?" my owner was asked when we reached the front of the line.

"Your basic mongrel."

"Not much demand for these, I'm afraid."

"She'll just have to take her chances."

"You're here to auction her?"

"Oh yes."

"Would you like a reserve price or should we just place her in the pool if she isn't sold?"

"The pool, I suppose," she said, with what sounded like reluctance.

"You can always change your mind. And how would you grade her behavior?"

"Having chosen the path of discipline but recently, she naturally needs further refinement in all areas. Also, due both to her relative age and the inherent obstreperousness of her personality, she requires a master of particularly firm, steady, and patient hand. On the other hand, she takes punishment exceedingly – perhaps even *excessively* – well."

"Very good. You can go now," said the other, in the distracted way of weary bureaucrats everywhere. I heard her stamp something. "Show this to the vet and have her do the usual tests."

We walked a little way, then my owner stopped. "The vet will take off your muzzle to check your teeth. Do not attempt to nip or bite her! It'll go on the report; you may be sure no one will want a pet who misbehaves in such a fashion."

While waiting on line at the 'vet's,' the owners discussed training methods ('reward' versus 'punishment'), new styles of leashes and muzzles and other restraints, nutritional supplements, etc. When my number was called I was forced onto a scale where my weight was taken, my height and breasts and hips measured, my reflexes checked. My muzzle was removed and I was ordered to open my mouth. "Lots of fillings, and I believe a canine tooth, of all things, is missing," said the dentist vet. "How old is she?"

"I don't know precisely. She came without identification of any kind."

"She's probably older than she looks," she said, pulling apart my jaws.

As my muzzle was off the questions could have been addressed directly to me, but the vet directed all questions to my owner.

"Considering her age, she's not in bad shape."

"Still, most people don't want dogs this age."

"I know," replied my owner. "She may very well end up in the pound."

"Of course, some people *do* prefer older dogs. Although set in their ways, they're less frisky and demanding of attention."

"That's not the case with her, as her training began extremely late."

After replacing the muzzle she poked my ribs and squeezed various parts of my anatomy, including my genitals and rectal area, where I was examined for genital warts, herpes, and hemorrhoids. Having been declared free of all diseases, I was permitted to proceed to the registration area, where I was assigned a number (#33); a card was attached to my collar listing my various dimensions and what they knew of my history. Then I heard a door open, and we entered an area that, judging by the sound of music, laughter, and canine noises, the smell of alcohol and cigarette and cigar and even marijuana smoke, seemed packed with people and animals.

My owner stopped just inside the door. "This is your chance to impress others with your sociability, your intelligence, and your obedience. If you know what is good for you, you will not disappoint me."

But I didn't feel like impressing anybody. I wanted only to be safe at 'home' – in my master's house, even if in a cage, and even if forced to perform various acts with Charlie. Indeed, I wished Charlie was here, no matter what I had to do with him.

What difference would it make, after all, if no one could recognize me? I began to whimper, and clung pathetically to my master, constantly entangling myself in her feet and thereby causing her great annoyance. Even when she even unleashed me and ordered me to go play with the other dogs, I refused to leave her side. At times, stopping to exchange gossip with the other owners, she ordered me to perform tricks, and my skills and deficiencies in these areas were compared to those of other animals, as if all of us were merely merchandise. "She's been here before, hasn't she?" someone asked.

"No, it's her first time at the auctions."

"But she looks so familiar...."

"All those years at the Duchess...."

"...Paula's...."

"...the piers...."

"Been looking for an owner long as I can remember, that's for sure...."

"...lucky someone took pity on her...."

"I've a soft heart," said my owner. Laughter.

"Has she been a great disappointment?"

"Not so much, though she *is* overly submissive. I prefer a bitch with a bit more spirit, actually."

"Perhaps she's just very attached to you."

"Of course. But I take no pride in it. She would have responded the same to anyone who owned her."

"That should stand her in good stead."

"Assuming someone wants her—"

"Luckily that's no longer my problem."

Surely all this was too elaborate for a mere joke. I collapsed onto the floor in a state of shock, and began to howl.

My owner grabbed me by the collar, dragged me a short distance away, then bent down and whispered harshly in my ear. "Understand," she said, "Our time together is over. This decision was made a long time ago, and there is nothing you can do to change it. You have nothing to reproach me for," she said, as I whimpered. "Our agreement was for a fixed amount of time and in that, as in all other things, I have thoroughly complied with the parameters agreed upon. Any further expectations that you have or have had are yours and yours alone. In any case, I have more than done my duty, and you have been prepared as well as could be expected in such a short period of time. By the end of the evening you will have your choice as to your future mode of life, either to continue in some fashion with what we have begun, or return to your former life. No matter what mode of existence you choose, it shall not be with me."

She then gave me a bone, which I ordinarily would have found succulent, but now refused to eat.

"Is she often off her feed?" someone asked.

"She was on her own for so long, she hasn't totally learned her true station," said my owner. "*Eat*," she ordered. "Behave yourself or no one will want you."

I felt myself blushing, as if I were being stared at, although it was consolation that my actual face was visible to no one. Finally, pretending I was Charlie, I opened my mouth. The bone was so large I could barely get my jaw around it, and the smell of the slightly rancid meat made me gag. Saliva spilled out of my mouth as I sucked on it, and a tiny piece of gristle kept tickling my nose.

Other dogs smelled the bone, and attempted to take it from me. Some seemed born dogs and others like me, or at least so

I surmised from the odors emanating from their mouths and skin, from the tickling and scratching of fur.

During this fighting over the food, several of the dogs had sniffed or even licked my genitalia, but I had managed to fend them off, to the amusement of those surrounding. But when I became engaged in a struggle with a huge dog, whose licks on my face were almost as repulsive as the thrusts of his penis, my owner ordered me to be receptive. I growled my disapproval.

"Shall we hold her down?" someone asked.

"Unnecessary," said my owner.

"She'll never obey you."

"She will. To demonstrate her love for me and ask for my pardon, so that I might be persuaded to keep her."

Was this a possibility? If so, it put things in a new light. Those around grew silent; even the huge dog stayed still, waiting for my response.

My future, I felt, was in my hands. Not that I utterly believed her, but what other hope did I have? So I let the dog lick my face, and push against me with his paws, and when I could feel his penis tickling me I rolled onto my stomach and raised my ass in the air, spreading my legs as far apart as my chains permitted to grant him easier access.

"See!" announced my owner, in triumph.

My gyrations were unnecessary, as the dog's penis was small and slipped so easily inside that I could barely feel it. I clutched my legs together to hold him there. He was panting loudly, but just before it seemed he would ejaculate he was pulled away from me, to the sound of great howling on his part.

"What a slut your bitch is," said someone.

"You don't even have to hold her legs open."

"See how she clasps that little pecker to her body…."

"…all my years never seen one like this."

To make sure I was 'impregnated,' other dogs, too numerous to count, were forced to mate with me, some so small they had to be held against my body, and others so large they crushed me to the floor. After a while I no longer noticed the catcalls and laughter, and found myself writhing in unison with my partners, out of desire or shame, I could not tell, but pants and cries around me assured me that others were engaged in similar behavior. Once all the animals had had their way with me, we lay together in an exhausted heap on the floor, my costume half torn off as the dogs sucked and munched my teats, till they lost interest or their owners called them away to service others….

Finally I was left alone, liquid dripping out of all my orifices, to the background music of grunts and high-pitched howls and bellows, and, as if from a great distance, the murmur of half-heard and but barely understood sentences:

"…first dog scene…."

"…not quite house trained…."

"…use the code word…use the code word," and laughter as it would or could not be used, and sobs afterwards so similar to mine.

"She's more experienced than you, but hasn't learned her lessons half as well," my owner whispered in my ear. "Indeed, you have done me proud. Had you been less so I would not have been able to dismiss you so readily…."

She walked away too quickly for me to follow.

85

Truly alone, I wandered among the others, who on occasion petted me or fed me a morsel or two, but just as often ignored me or shooed me away.

"...not very well-behaved, is she?"

"...once even went to the apartment...."

"...no wonder she's being abandoned."

"...who can stand such possessiveness...?"

"...even loyalty can go too far...."

"...like love, anything can become a burden...."

"...don't remind me of poor Chouzhoo...."

"...you were terribly cruel, Mariella...."

"And what am I do, pray tell, when a pet begins to pee on my furniture and shit on my bed, all because I prefer some other to her – when she attacks my other animals, and destroys their toys? Who is the owner here, and who the slave?"

"Did you ever find out what became of her?"

"The new owner, I believe, took her down south. I think she wanted to use her to herd sheep."

"That's difficult work. Wasn't she a bit long in the tooth?"

"She was younger than she looked. Of course, if it doesn't work out...."

Laughter drowned out the last part of this sentence. I wondered if it were a human canine they were talking about, or a 'real' dog – or if this was even a 'real' conversation, or something they used to scare me and the others?

"Perhaps it's not a good idea to talk about it here...."

"They still understand English?"

"*Naturellement*. Just because one cannot speak—"

"But faculties that are unused become withered, surely."

"Over time, yes, but we're talking years…."

"What about the—"

"That was a terrible story."

"Pneumonia, wasn't it? A very cold winter."

"Louisa's always worked her dogs too hard. Her turnover is astonishing."

"I'd hate to be bid on by her."

"She better start being more careful. There's been too much talk."

"It's a huge preserve, though."

"And very beautiful, so I hear."

"You've never been there?"

"Not yet, but we've been invited for Mastiff Homecoming."

"*That* is something. You should try to make it. I wouldn't miss it for the world."

"If Becky can arrange time off from work."

"Depends on my boss."

"Bring her." Laughter.

"It's not only mastiffs, is it?"

"Oh no. That's just the name. Almost all breeds allowed, except—"

"What about that trouble we kept hearing about? It's completely taken care of?"

"Some deal with the wardens."

"Money—"

"I still don't believe—"

"It's true. You know that bitch of Marty's? When Marty got tired of her she sold her to Louisa—"

"I *liked* that bitch. I would've bought her if I'd known."

"As if I would have let you!"

"*Girls*! Not in front—"

"They'll find out soon enough."

"Better later than sooner."

"...not like it's not consensual."

"What does that matter? They're just *animals*. They don't care."

"They care. They're sentient beings just like us."

"Not 'just' like us."

"Face it, gals – Hitler was loved by his dog."

"Did Hitler even have a dog?"

There was a fanfare and the room fell silent, then a voice made deeper and more resonant by the sound of a loudspeaker commenced to speak: "The annual meeting of the Society of the Leash is about to commence. All animals must immediately be leashed, and those not participating brought to the kennels or the dog run. Participating animals should be on stage in five minutes in preparation for the viewing."

This announcement relieved me. Surely now my owner would come fetch me.

Around me was instant confusion: owners whistling for their pets, the clankings of leashes being dropped on the floor, cages being opened and shut, the reiteration of last-minute instructions, even a few pathetic animals begging their owners, in English (for which they were immediately punished), for yet another chance.

My owner did not appear. As much as I'd resented being consigned to my cage, I would have given anything for the sanctuary of it now, or even that of what she had referred to as the 'dog run.' Crouched on my paws, I rested immobile, as if by not moving I could become invisible.

86

"There's a stray here," someone called.

"She's clearly a pet, she belongs to . . . ."

A name was about to be uttered, but there was a loud "shhh."

"She's clearly been abandoned."

"What number is she?" shouted the voice in the megaphone.

I felt my collar being grabbed. "33. She's not even groomed."

"It doesn't matter. Bring her up immediately."

I tried to run, but hands grabbed me and, despite my kicking, managed to attach a leash to my collar. I longed for the familiar voices that had mocked me in the van, or even for those I had come to know as "Louisa" or "Mariella." But I recognized no voice, and heard no familiar name.

"If you keep this up, no one will take you," warned the person holding me.

"Or they'll send you out west, for the secondary auctions."

"If she's a stray, how come they just don't let her go?"

Sighs, and the sound represented by "tsk."

"They might. But she'll probably end up in the pound anyway. They have a tough time, you know. One or two made their way back, so I've heard, but Cheryl says that's just a rumor, to discourage us from abandoning them."

"Shouldn't this be resolved before the auction begins?"

"What do you suggest?"

"I think we should ask. That way we're protected if there's any problems."

"What kind of problems?"

"Like the police—"

"Of course she'll be *missed*. People just don't disappear—"

"I don't see why, if nobody wants her—"

"Look, I'm not opposed. If it was up to me, I wouldn't have any penalties for the breaking of contracts. Even degradation soon loses its savor, unless it's continually chosen—"

"But there are moments in every contract when the animal would escape if she could. If there aren't, I believe you could argue the master isn't doing her job."

"On the contrary. If there *are*, the master isn't doing her job."

"*Between* sessions, anyway. But don't you agree things should always be terminated at the point when desire is inflamed rather than satiated?"

"In an *ideal* relationship – yes. But how many, even of—"

"It's up to us, as the knowledgeable ones, to make the relationship ideal. Once initial acquiescence is obtained, it's just a matter of rhythm and pace. And the longer it continues the less important even *those* are. It's the the the lack of challenge, ultimately, that's so boring…."

"*Places*." The gavel struck. I was dragged to the stage.

We who were to be auctioned were lined up, with short leashes linking us collar to collar. A second fanfare sounded, and the voice proclaimed: "Here it is, what we've all been waiting for, the Presentation of the Bitches." I had no way of knowing how many of us there were, but judging by the jostling and the sounds of other bodies, there were perhaps fifteen or twenty dogs.

In a kind of parade we were led around the room – heeling, pointing, jumping, etc. at a command from our ringleader – accompanied by a stream of laughter, jokes, and snide asides from those in the room.

After perhaps fifteen minutes, when the parade had petered out to catcalls and whistles, we were led back onto the stage, where, our collars detached from each other and a portion of our costumes removed, a more personal "show period" commenced, as those who were interested in obtaining a pet were invited to examine us at closer range.

Asses in air, heads on our paws, the auctioneer traversed the line, outlining our assets and deficiencies and inviting others to do the same. When it came to me the auctioneer noted that I was an aging bitch, clearly past my prime, once attractive, perhaps, but clearly no longer so, and as the parts of my body were positioned for close inspection she illustrated my deficiencies – wrinkles and scars and liver spots, hairs sprouting from places they never used to, and the sagging of my belly from middle-aged paunch. In my defense, she added that I might be presumed to possess some of that wisdom age is known to confer, as well as the gentleness (or was it exhaustion?) of those who had experienced much of the vicissitudes of life. Additional jokes were made at my expense, in the vein of earlier ones, to which I quickly ceased paying attention. I was examined internally as well: fingers entered various orifices as others yanked my teats, flicked my clitoris, or strove to dig wax and mucus out of my nose and ears.

All this was painful, of course, and humiliating, but at least it was *personal*, and to that extent I welcomed it.

87

The auction itself commenced. "Muffy is a well-trained and beloved dog, whose owner is forced to part with her as she is moving to a building that will not accept pets. She is prone to digestive problems, and needs frequent walking...." The auctioneer reminded everyone that permission was needed from the club for breeding purposes, that the probationary period had been extended to three months, and – most important! – that owning a dog was a great responsibility and if there were any doubts at all it was a duty best not undertaken. The bidding for Muffy was desultory, and a provisional owner might more honestly be said to have volunteered rather than bought her.

Next was "Flora" – a "Weimaraner look-alike" animal who was extolled for her long silky hair and strong legs. Her former owner (who unfortunately had to return to her country of birth) commanded her to do a special stunt, which she did (of course I did not know what it was) to a large amount of cheering. The bidding was prolonged and competitive, and finally settled to great applause.

Eventually the sale of those who had previously been pets and hence were used to their status was completed, and a short break was announced. "It's your turn next," the auctioneer warned me. "The most important moment of your life is here. Only if you remain calm and clearheaded, with an open heart and mind, will you know what the right thing is for you to do."

With the drumroll the room gained an air of palpable anticipation and excitement. "It is now time for the most exciting event of the evening – the sale of the novices. We have only one with us tonight, described by her former owner as obstinate and willful, prone to biting and other forms of disobedience, but also capable of deep attachment." There was the rustling of paper. "This mongrel responds particularly well to corporal punishment, the severer the better." To illustrate, there was a whopping hit with a cane on my thighs, to which I disdained responding to, even by a moan. Hoots and whistles came from the crowd, and some ironic-sounding "bravos." Someone shouted that I'd be a fine match for Alicia, and there were calls for "Alicia…Alicia…."

"Thanks, my friends, for your kind testimony as to my prowess in the martial areas," said (I assume) the one named Alicia. "But I've closed my kennels for the moment – at least until my rotator cuffs are back to normal." Laughter.

"Come come," said the auctioneer, banging with her gavel. "Let us proceed in a tone appropriate to the most sacred of our rituals."

At these words the room instantly quieted, so that you could not even hear the lowering of a glass upon a table. The auctioneer then turned to me and addressed the following words:

"You have demonstrated knowledge of the rudimentary commands, without which, according to the rules of our organization, you would not have been permitted to proceed to the Magnificent Choice. The Magnificent Choice is the sacred heart of our society, that which makes all else possible. Without you and those like you, our organization could not exist, as, in a wholly different way, without us and those like us you could not exist, at least not in the form you most desire. Indeed, all of us in this room have, in the manner appropriate to our roles, stood in front of this group and proclaimed our allegiance to our order.

"Be aware, however, that once a decision is made, it is irrevocable – both for those like you, who have been permitted to make the Magnificent Choice, and those like me, who have been granted the privilege – and burden – of being able to confer such an opportunity on you. The rule binds us forever, and commences immediately, with no time for goodbyes or tidying up loose ends in one's former life. Few are those who, having joined us, later desire to return to the other world, but for the safety of our order

and those in it we cannot permit this. Indeed, we consider ourselves not just a group of individuals, but guardians of a certain
mode of life, more ancient than any of us, whose history, if you
become one of us, you will eventually be taught.

"For the safety of all, then, the decision is final, nor can we
permit you to communicate in any form with what would be
considered your past, lest you attempt to conceal messages or
secret codes in letters or wills or testaments. Not that as yet we
have found such constraints to be necessary, but the necessity
of protecting our society requires that we overlook no means of
ensuring our safety. That is why it is imperative you must decide,
from your brain and your heart, of course, but perhaps most
importantly from your soul, as to what you truly desire. Those
who choose this life must be decisive and courageous: there is
no room for recriminations or regrets! We have the means – do
not disturb yourself as to how – to terminate your bank accounts,
your credit cards, your electric and utility bills, to empty your
apartment of all that is in it. Notes will be sent and actions
undertaken to ensure that those who might be disturbed by
your disappearance will not attempt to search for you, let alone
'rescue' you. Indeed, your 'case' will be disposed of, in a manner
as painless as possible, so that thoughts of you shall not long
trouble those left behind.

"As your possessions will be destroyed, so too will all forms
of identification be eradicated from your body. Any attempt to
escape will be met with the severest of penalties – not necessarily
what you think, by the way, for there are penalties worse than
the obvious. Indeed, banishment from the pack, a solitary life as
a stray, is generally considered far worse than being mutilated or
'put away.' As a member of the pack, you shall belong entirely

to us – although not *necessarily* or at least *always* to a particular master – but you will have a place as a member of a group to which you have by choice and by nature desired to belong, that is aware of your history and your desires, that honors your choices and commitments and absolves you forever of the tedious curse of humanhood. No more jobs, no more taxes, no more checkbooks, no more bills, no more credit cards, no more credit, no more money, no more mortgages, no more rent, no more savings, no more junk mail, no more junk, no more mail, no more phones, no more faxes, no more busy signals, no more computers, no more cars, no more drivers' licenses, no more traffic lights, no more airports, no more flying, no more tickets, no more packing, no more luggage, no more supermarkets, no more health clubs, no more washing, no more ironing, no more vacuuming, no more sweeping, no more shaving, no more toothpaste, no more dental floss, no more vitamins, no more lipstick, no more makeup, no more shrinks, no more elevators, no more subways, no more subway tokens, no more health insurance, no more medical forms, no more situps, no more Q-tips, no more pin numbers, no more cooking, no more dieting, no more plant watering, no more painting, no more polishing, no more sanding, no more varnishing, no more replacing lightbulbs, no more haircuts, no more shoes, no more nose picking, no more nail clippers, no more nail files, no more nail polish, no more hammers, no more to-do lists, no more watches, no more alarm clocks, no more art, no more arguments, no more Thanksgivings, no more Christmas, no more presents, no more buying, no more 'thank yous,' no more 'pleases,' no more sucking up, no more lying, no more arguments, no more 'no mores'.... Not that you will never take a shower or have your ears checked for mites, but that you will no longer have the responsibility for doing such. Though you do nothing to earn a living, you will be fed, you will be groomed, you will be housed.

"And many of the constraints currently upon you will be no more. Immediately upon being accepted as a member of the group, your blindfold will be removed and you will be returned to the world of sight.

"On the other hand, should you decide such an existence is not for you, you may choose to leave us and return to the life you used to lead. Once you decide this, all physical punishments will immediately cease, your clothing will be returned to you, and within a short amount of time you will be transported to within a walking distance of your home. No one will try to dissuade of your choice, and no one outside this arena need be any the wiser. Indeed, from that moment forth, all restraints will be removed, save those sufficient to ensure you remain blindfolded and unknowing of whom your masters are, and you shall return to what is considered 'freedom' – with all the pleasures – and weights and duties and obligations and responsibilities – that this entails.

"But remember, irrevocable as the decision to stay is, equally irrevocable is the decision to leave. Due to our aforementioned concerns about the safety of our group and ways of secretly retaining contact with the so-called 'normal world,' this opportunity comes only once, before it can be anticipated and prepared for and perhaps, even, undermined. A choice not to join us now is a choice to remove yourself from us forever, and things will not go well for you if you attempt to betray whatever of our secrets you think you possess. Do not think your silly subterfuges at disguise and so forth have in any way prevented us from knowing who you are. If you betray us, revenge may not be swift, but it is certain, and your knowledge is insufficient, in any case, to harm us. You may be sure we are not without connections.

"You should also understand that, should you join our society and offer yourself up to auction, it is possible that no one may care to purchase you – as, naturally, most prospective owners prefer animals younger and more appealing than yourself. In the back of the room are cages, not just for dogs whose owners are on vacation, but strays who have as yet to find a home. Unlike, however, the so-called 'animal welfare' organizations in the human world, we never dispose of unwanted animals except in cases of extreme age and disease, when it is clear, from the expression in the eyes, that the time has come. No, you will have a place with us until someone is willing to adopt you and take you into their home, and, if not, you will be exercised and groomed and fed and be able to enjoy the companionship of other canines in a fashion that animals in an ordinary kennel could only envy.

"On occasion, although quite rarely, when a dog is adopted, the arrangement for some reason or other does not work out, and the pet may be returned to the shelter to await another home. The first three months are considered a probation period, during which an owner may return a pet at any time, for any reason whatsoever. After that, the ruling committee decides whether a return is justified, and fines or other punishments may be levied on those who go against our rulings.

"Luckily, these warnings are almost always unnecessary. Most of our animals have no trouble finding adoption, and in general there is an easy fit between a pet and its master. Occasionally, however, owners of the newly trained, such as yourself, find the pet in need of greater discipline or instruction than they them-selves are able to impart, and for those we offer special classes.

Adjustment is usually made within a month or two.

"Let me reiterate, however, that regardless of what happens once you have joined the pack, even should you be so unfortunate as to have to spend the rest of your life in a cage, initiation into the Society – which includes physical marks and other alterations – will ensure that you will be utterly incapable of returning to the world you have chosen to abandon. By the rules of our society I cannot tell you precisely what these alterations are, but initially they almost always result in enormous pain, rage and regret on the part of whosoever undergoes them, in part because they are irrevocable, and in part because (as the vocal chords are severed and fingers and thumb sewn together like paws), the initiated is no longer capable of expressing herself in the verbal and written fashions to which those in our culture have become accustomed. This is profoundly upsetting to everyone, of course, but it will be especially so to one such as yourself, whose previous life consisted largely of the recounting of her experiences and feelings – both in your former mode of employment as well as in countless conversations with friends and members of the so-called 'therapeutic community.' But you should also be aware that, *regardless of whether you consider yourself able to express it*, all of us will know and understand and be able to empathize with what you are feeling. Indeed, we have come to consider such rage and regret a normal reaction to the cessation of one's former life – a necessary precursor, indeed, to the start of the new. Some are more attached to their old life than others, and of course these suffer more. But this mourning is not only necessary, it is something you will come to be grateful for, as you will be for the physical changes separating your old self from the new. Because the sooner you understand –

and by *you* I mean your *body* as well as your *brain* – there is no going back – the sooner you will accept your new way of being and be content with the life you have chosen.

"Though you will never talk again, or communicate in any fashion through what is generally considered 'language,' you will be able to express your needs and wants in a manner that ensures your obtaining the care you need. You will have the companionship of others like yourself, the animal comfort of their bodies, food and other sustenance, and the luxury of having no obligations or worries. And that is the worst case scenario.

"But there are greater things to which you may aspire. Assuming that you have taken your training seriously, that you have studied well the ways in which to obey and serve your masters, that you have renounced the parts of yourself that are now useless and embraced those that make you more animal-like, almost surely you will obtain the protection and affection of a personal Owner, one will be as bound to you as you are to her – and in that bond between those who order and those who obey, in the mutual recognition of Otherness and Oneness, in that inchoate but profound understanding that only develops between those who must communicate without language, you will achieve a position few in this world ever know – one that is both wholly slave and wholly free, wholly vulnerable and wholly safe, wholly arbitrary and wholly guaranteed. For though love between humans dies, who has ever heard of such happening between human and animal? Almost surely you will be transported to wilderness areas of great recreational possibilities where you will learn to retrieve birds and catch rodents, you will lie on the floor on cold winter nights at the feet of your master, warmed by the fire, extravagantly petted and praised. When you are old and no longer able to climb up stairs you will be given a warm basket by the kitchen, when you are unable to serve you will be placed in the kennel with other animals, when you are ill and dying you will be put to sleep in a manner so unexpected and painless that any human might envy it. One thing only is required of you, and that is to do what your master commands. And already you know how easy this is, you have been doing so the past few months. No memory is required, no complications, no logistics, no planning, no time constraints. For in this world there is no worry or anxiety or envy or despair. Why worry when one's wants are anticipated? How be anxious when there is no choice to be made? How envy when you have chosen your lot? How despair in a world where every directive provides meaning?

"And now," the auctioneer addressed the room, "that this aging bitch may make as informed a choice as possible as to the future mode of her existence, that she may choose with as much knowledge as possible of what our world is like, I must ask all of you to put on your masks."

There was a period of shuffling, then, to my astonishment, the muzzle was taken off my tongue and the covering removed from my eyes.

I had grown so accustomed to the dark that the light at first only blinded me; I had to shut my eyes against the glare. And indeed, a bright light was shining in my face, as if to ensure the world around me remained in shadow.

When my eyes became adjusted the first thing I noticed was the auctioneer, encased in a little spotlight to the front and right of me. Of imposing height and substantial girth, elegantly attired in a deconstructed tuxedo of the sort favored by the more outré Japanese designers, and sporting a buzzcut and neatly trimmed beard, the initial impression the auctioneer gave was of being of the male gender, yet it was quickly quite clear (perhaps from some humorous lines about her mouth, or the positioning of her torso on her legs – less casual and sprawling than that of men) that her gender was female. She wore mirrored sunglasses instead of a mask. There was something familiar about her that disturbed and reassured me in approximately equal measure.

As she approached, I saw reflected in her spectacles an animal I had never seen before. It moved as I did, but still, it took me several seconds to realize it was me. It had neither the shape nor color I had expected, yet it suited me perfectly, far more so than if had I chosen it myself, yet I could not tell you its breed.

Only the largest dogs, of course, approached my size, but whereas the bodies of Great Danes and St. Bernards were concentrated in their torsos and thick necks and powerful jaws, my weight was distributed more equally over a frame far less muscular, in flesh that was fattier and of much less density than that of my canine cousins. Although my limbs were longer, I could not run as quickly on my four legs (or even two) as they could on their thinner but stronger ones. My coat was shorter than I had imagined, and the fur somewhat bushier, standing straight out like the ruff of a Husky. My face was wide with a longish snout, on top of which white bristles extended in a rather elegant arc.

The stage on which I stood was surrounded on three sides by mirrors, and the parts of my body I had been trying most to hide were clearly exposed to the audience. They sat below me in darkness, in a large room from which emanated vague grunt-ings and sighs, snufflings and snorts, as if one were in a jungle surrounded by wild animals and birds.

As I stared out, I became aware of little points of light, which

I gradually realized were candles. These illuminated only dimly a large, industrial-looking space, perhaps an old factory or wholesale butcher's, with huge metal shutters covering what I supposed were the openings. Toward the side was some old rusted machinery whose function I could not discern.

But it was the occupants of the room who most interested me. Out of the dimness bodies began to emerge: thick and thin, short and tall, dressed in an astonishing variety of costume. Some were in tuxedos and formal dresses, others in sports jackets and merino jacket-and-skirt ensembles, others in faded levis and leather boots – but all with black masks over their eyes to conceal their identities. Standing mutely but elegantly by their sides were others in costumes like mine that mimicked the canines of various breeds, from aristocratic Russian Wolfhounds to swift Rhodesian Ridgebacks to lumbering Newfoundland retrievers. There were bulldogs from England, and water dogs from Portugal, and terriers from Scotland. There were cuddly sheepdogs and earnest pointers, sad-eyed hounds and overdressed poodles, friendly spaniels and elegant setters, plus a scattering of such overbred creatures as Shih Tzu, Shiba inu, and Bouvier des Flandres. Some were blindfolded, as I had been, but others stared at me on their haunches with bright curious eyes.

"Behold," the auctioneer said, "the Society of the Leash. Before making your decision, it is imperative that you wander amongst us with your eyes open, that you step into our cages and witness how our animals live, so that you may never reproach us or yourself for not having been given an understanding of who and what we are. As you are observing us we of course are observing *you*, to judge if you are indeed worthy of being welcomed into our Society."

Ever since the unveiling of my eyes there had been perfect silence, as all present studied my reactions without expression. I felt paralyzed and, unable in other ways to express myself, began to howl, and an answering howl went around the room.

"This walk is not necessary, of course, if you are absolutely certain that our way of life is not for you. If such is the case, you may retreat to the rear of the stage, where our handlers will bring you back as quickly as possible to what is considered the real world."

I quieted myself, though I remained incapable of movement. After some minutes of this, the auctioneer motioned the handlers to approach me, but as they neared I backed away – not because I was uncertain as to what choice I would make, but from an overwhelming curiosity. Such a life – if you could even call it such – was of course not for me, but what harm could it do to linger, to discover what manner of creature inhabited this room, either as 'owner' or 'animal' people who, for all I knew, I had sat next to in school, been interviewed by for a job, danced with in a bar, people who perchance had sold me groceries, replaced my fillings, polished my floor, were ex-lovers or shrinks to whom I'd confided the secrets of my heart. Did I not owe it to myself, as a writer – or even a human with the standard human concerns – to witness what I could of this peculiar universe before eternally bidding it *adieu*? Therefore, in the free and open spirit of scientific inquiry, I approached the steps of the stage and cumbersomely descended on all fours into the room.

Behind the masks, eyes glittered. The room was warm, and as my costume permitted little airflow, I began to pant. When water was offered I was glad enough to avail myself of it, though it was in a bowl on the floor. Lost in thought, wondering which of those present was my owner (if indeed she were still there), I was roused out of my guzzling by a low growl. Water dripping off my jowls (for by habit I continued to let my jaw hang open, even in the absence of the metal tongue restraint), I raised my head to find myself confronting the bared teeth of an Akita, who certainly would have attacked me had he (or she) not been constrained by a leash. Although decades of living in the world had only augmented my natural cynicism, I was nonetheless taken aback by this evidence of species betrayal. I would have assumed that the bond of sympathy between the dogs in this room would have transcended our obligations to our owners, and I bared my teeth in a growl.

"Down!" I heard, in what was unmistakably my master's voice. I immediately glanced around, hoping somehow to recognize her. Of course I could not, but I raced toward the table from where I thought her voice had come, gazing deeply into each masked face, but there was none whose features or size matched the image I had formed in my brain. Nor did their expressions provide any clue, for they stared at me impassively as I examined them, flickering not even an eyelash in response. In desperation I crawled under the table and sniffed their feet, hoping to identify my owner by her smell. But as I did not possess the sense of smell inherent to the canine born, I could not tell who amongst those sitting in utter silence and immobility was the one whom I had known so well.

"Resume your walk or return to the stage," I heard through the megaphone. Outwardly I abandoned the search, but continued surreptitiously to seek her, for it seemed possible that this apparent abandonment was just one more in the long series of Tests she had presented, to determine whether I was worthy of her eternal guardianship and love.

As I approached the rear of the room where the cages were, the dogs set up an eerie kind of howl. They stood at the front of their kennels, facing me, eyes expectant, mouths open, tongues hanging, and though my stomach revolted in disgust and shame, I found myself having to use all my willpower to resist joining in their cries.

The cages were clean and neat, full of food and drink, and roomy enough for the manner of animal in them. The door of one was open, and, thinking it unoccupied, I entered, in hopes of gaining a few moments of reflection free from the gaze of those outside. But I soon saw, in the rear, a large and beautifully groomed Husky, who, after cursorily sniffing my genitals, lay back on the floor with an indifference I found unnerving. Other than Charlie, I had spent little time with other canines, and it took awhile before it occurred to me (as it had occurred to me in social situations involving humans rather than animals) that the niceties of social interaction were the responsibility not just of my partner but also of myself. Upon realizing this I immediately made my way to the Husky and began to sniff and lick what turned out to be *her* genitals, after which we began to play together as old companions – rolling together on the ground, baring our teeth in displays of fighting, biting, chasing, etc. How long we enjoyed ourselves I cannot say – only that the drumroll eventually sounded, interrupting our games.

"Your time is up," the microphone boomed, and through the door of the cage a spotlight fell on me. I slowly made my way back to the stage, still examining faces behind the masks in hopes of discovering if not my owner, then at least someone I had known in my previous life.

"Do you have any questions?" the auctioneer asked.

There were hundreds, of course, but what was the point, for surely the important ones would not be answered. Nor, perhaps, *could* be answered, for I was not sure that what I wanted to know was in fact knowable, at least in a manner that could be communicated from one person to another.

"Note the shyness of the bitch," the auctioneer said. "It is the mark of someone who desires to acquiesce, but is ashamed of her desires."

"Where is my owner?" I finally asked.

I had not used language in so long, it was difficult to speak: not just to utter the syllables, but even to know what words to use. I scarcely recognized my voice

"What does it matter? She has abandoned you," the auctioneer replied.

"Why?"I cried.

"Why does anyone abandon anyone? That is the mystery of bodies."

"But I need to speak to her – to find out what to do."

"What is in question at the moment is not her desire, but yours. But of course" – she turned to the room – "the true slave is *unable* to perceive her desires, save as they relate to fulfilling the desires of another."

I made a sound – it came out like a bark – of protest and surprise. What had my entire life been about, if not the creation and appeasement of desire? Why had I answered the ad, if not to appease the strange stirrings in my body?

But as laughter, accompanied by what seemed a thumping of tails, went around the room, I realized that what she said was indeed true. My desire was not a true desire – an activity one could, in a pinch, pay someone to perform – but it was a desire to have someone else treat me a certain way, a way that would involve pain and humiliation, surely, but in a manner I myself did not choose, for to choose it was not my desire.

Shame spread through me, for who I was and that others should know – but also a kind of relief, in that I was at last understood.

"See how the abject creature bows her head in embarrassment. You see before you not the proud submission of the canine, but the craven cowardice of the human mongrel." I barked in protest. "She still resists her fate, as if all of us in this room do not know who she is – as if, indeed, many of us are not just like her. The bitch seems surprised at this," the auctioneer continued, "as if the existence of our group and countless others like us serves to mitigate her shame, as if, were she alone in her perversion, it would in any way invalidate her desires."

And indeed, I had slunk back on my haunches, my head buried in my paws, in a manner that the auctioneer pointed out was typical of canines.

"This will not do," she continued. "You must make your choice, in as clear and loud a voice as possible, so that all may hear and acknowledge your choice. Join our Society, or leave us forever. Which is it to be?"

As the bugle sounded a final three times, I thought of the Current and the boredom of our relations, then I thought of the one before the Current, and the one before that and the ones before that – those whom I had loved who had loved me in return, those for whom love had died in me faster than it had in them and those in whom love had died faster than in me, those whom I had loved who had never loved me no matter how much

I had wanted them to, and those I had never been able to bring myself to love, no matter how they had wanted me to and no matter how, in a perfect world, I would have been able to do so. I thought of those I had lived with for years, and those I had dated for months, and those I had embraced once for ten minutes within the locked bathroom of a bar, and all I saw was pain. Pain for love that had died and was no more, pain for love that had never been and never would be, and, most of all, pain for the pain I had suffered and would suffer again, because, after all, it is the nature of desire to go forever unfulfilled....

"You shake your head. I take it, then, you do not wish to join our Society?"

Unable to speak, I again shook my head.

"As you still reside in the Realm of Language and are not yet dependent on others to interpret your needs and desires, you must take responsibility – at least one final time – for who you are and proclaim it unequivocally, in full view and hearing of the microphones and camera, so that your choice may be recorded for all posterity. If you refuse or find yourself 'incapable' of speech, if you do not specifically announce your intentions to become one of us, we must assume your desire to leave, and deal with you accordingly." She waited several second, then clapped her hands; two women who had been standing at the side of the stage marched over to me. They yanked me to my feet, flung the mask over my eyes, and placed me in darkness once again.

But it was a different darkness than I had become accustomed to – one not in which anything might happen, but one from which all possibilities had been removed. A hand on each arm, stumbling (for I was not used to supporting myself with only two limbs) I felt myself being led off the stage – not to the sound of jeering and boos, as I would have expected, but utter silence.

Automatically, out of that resistance from which I had functioned my entire life, I pushed against those hands, fell down on all fours, dug in my paws, and refused to move.

The dogs in the audience started howling, and I began to howl too.

"Speak now, or forever hold your peace!" the auctioneer shouted.

"*No!*" I heard myself howl, then "*yes, yes, yes,*" as I took my irrevocable oaths, from different angles and closeups, with depth of field and telephoto, in profile and full face, immediately after which, in fulfillment of her warning, the muscles of my tongue and vocal chords were partially severed, so that I lost the capability of coherent speech. And I howled in pain and rage and regret, as she had foreseen, and – as she had also foreseen – as time passed I learned not just to accept my fate, but to embrace it with body, brain, and soul – so much so that, in memory of who I once had been and in trust of whom I had become, I was allowed, before my fingers were fully converted to paws, to record my story: partly for the benefit of those who had known me personally, so that they may cease torturing themselves over the nature of my so-called 'disappearance,' but mostly to alert those like us who are unaware of our existence about a world in which, if they are lucky, they may someday find themselves at home.

But all that came later, after I had abandoned the world of words for another – one deeper and richer, surely, with its own joys and sorrows – but of this, alas, I cannot speak.

THE END

Printed in the United States
by Baker & Taylor Publisher Services